Seven Shifts

a novella

Janet Parker Vaughan

Cover: Rebekah Wetmore
Author image: Brenda Barry

Editor: Andrew Wetmore

ISBN: 978-1-9992687-2-5
First edition August, 2020

397 Parker Mountain Road
Granville Ferry NS
B0S 1A0

moosehousepress.com
info@moosehousepress.com

We live and work in Mi'kma'ki, the ancestral and unceded territory of the Mi'kmaq People. This territory is covered by the "Treaties of Peace and Friendship" which Mi'kmaq and Wolastoqiyik (Maliseet) People first signed with the British Crown in 1725. The treaties did not deal with surrender of lands and resources but in fact recognized Mi'kmaq and Wolastoqiyik (Maliseet) title and established the rules for what was to be an ongoing relationship between nations. We are all Treaty people.

Acknowledgements

Seven Shifts appears in the light of day through the unfailing love and encouragement of friends.

From the beginning Elaine Bird and Carrie Walker-Jones expressed faith in my writing, and in the process of Seven Shifts as it was being written.

When I moved back to Nova Scotia, members of the Authors' Ink group in Middleton were helpful and supportive listeners.

New friends Anne Pollett and Marilyn Durling read the manuscript and gave me confidence in what I was about. Donna Burton, new friend, gave helpful advice.

Sandra Barry, poet, scholar and friend, not only first edited the manuscript, but brought a heightened awareness to the cultural and psychological nature of the shifts as they reveal Maree's development in her time and place.

Janet Barkhouse, poet and friend, in her reading of the manuscript immediately felt that Maree's story was unique. She drove across the province on a hot July day to meet with me and to insist that *Seven Shifts* must be published. Not only that, she said that a kaleidoscope should grace the cover. It does.

To all of you, dear friends, my heartfelt gratitude.

I also have to thank George Elliott Clarke who heard part of the manuscript at one of his workshops and gave it unqualified encouragement.

In particular, I thank Andrew Wetmore, editor at Moose House Publications, for his refined attention, his suggestions, his great sense of fun. I also give huge thanks to Rebekah Wetmore, artist, for her design of an especially beautiful cover.

To my daughter, Suzy Parker, who sees me through each day with support and lovely meals and literary advice, as always my abiding love and gratitude.

Foreword

Seven Shifts is about the mystery and puzzle of perception: how we begin to see, understand and integrate the world around us; how we are changed by the myriad experiences of childhood; how we emerge and evolve into our own story, mythology. Though perceived by a specific child in a specific place and time, transformed by imagination and language, this re-visioning of powerful memories reaches far beyond any specificity. It resonates on multiple frequencies and reminds us what it meant to discover moments, people, events and objects that altered us irrevocably.

In *Seven Shifts* we see how we are in relation to our environment (natural, domestic, social, cultural) and to others (family, friends, strangers, teachers), but most importantly we learn how we are in relation to ourselves.

Lyrical, sensory, impressionistic, tonal, Seven Shifts creates a sensation that reveals not so much a losing of innocence (though there is that, too), but a finding of wisdom. There are gifts and dangers in revelation; the child's response to this paradox in *Seven Shifts* is the essence of becoming a human being.

Sandra Barry
author of
Elizabeth Bishop: Nova Scotia's "Home-Made" Poet

This book is lovingly dedicated to my late husband
Edward Richard Vaughan,
priest and story teller.

Table of contents

Janet Parker Vaughan

First Shift

—age three to four—

This my new bed. A bed without bars. Where this summer night I lie in whole sight of the plaster ceiling and its slant of pink-striped wallpaper, lie with wide open eyes staring at deer-heads, small figures with beige faces and golden antlers that are in the stripes and around the border of the wallpaper. Deer-heads that see the whole sight of me. Stare down at me with understanding.

Long evenings of summer, peaceful, in this my new bed. Where, when I am not staring at the deer, I gaze toward the window and its drawn blind, watch behind it the orange glow of sunset, its change to gentle dimness, to dusk. A dusk in which I lie patiently, wait with open eyes to spin out into the wallpaper just before it turns to blackness.

I am older this summer. I know because of the bed. Its curved ends of cold brown metal tubes and its slumped mattress and its pillows of shallow feathers that are slinky soft. Grown-up bed in which I am sleeping alone, in which I learn, to keep myself from sinking, how to put my arms out over the quilt, out over the dry white edge of the sheet.

All summer in my new bed sleeping peacefully alone. But in winter, not alone. Because my mother comes in from her room to sleep with me. Has to. "I have to," she says. Because of asthma attacks.

On the nights I wheeze, she gets into my bed on the far side, bending her head along the slant of the ceiling. Gets in with a weight that slumps the mattress deeply, making me feel as if I am on a steep side-hill and about to slide. Gets in and slumps the bed and pulls the layers of heavy quilts up as far as she can to almost cover our heads. Making us hot, very hot. Hot like a furnace-hot hole. I, on my sidehill, try not to disappear, not to slide, with my feet braced against her thigh. So to try to go to sleep, heaving for air against the hot weight of the quilts. Heave for air or die.

Sometimes, to breathe easier and not to lie crosswise, I turn, face away from my mother, cling to the edge of the mattress, stick my leg out into the cold room, bend it back over the cotton of the quilt so my foot feels safe and cool and clean. But when I do this she always gets up, stumbles along the wall's darkened slant, goes around the end of the bed to turn on the light.

"What is this foot doing sticking out!" she scolds, tucking it back in.

After she says this I wait. I wait until she turns off the light, goes back around the end of the bed, bends along the wall, weighs down the mattress, pulls the covers back over our heads, wait until she is settled and asleep again. Then I put out a hand. In this way I learn to breathe through either foot or hand.

But I like it when my mother sleeps with me. Even though the bed feels heavy and thick. I like it that she is there for company while I am sick. I like it she is there to change my soaking pyjamas, to put on more Vicks. I like it, my mother looking after me.

"I don't want to see you choke to death while you're asleep," is what she says.

I like it, too, when she leaves the room in the morning, when I can lie face up again, more on a level, when I can raise my arms in fresh pyjama sleeves over the edge of the sheet. I like it when I am left alone, asthma over and wheezing softly, to weakly dry out in coolness and peace.

Some nights when it is very cold, my mother tells me to keep my head under the quilts, not to breathe the frosty air. It is on these nights that I stay awake a long time, my nose at the very edge of a black unknown. I am not afraid. I know when I wake up in the morning, my mother will get up, bend along the slant of the wall, go to the window to exclaim about the deep white forests of frost that coat the panes.

Sometimes, when I am getting over an attack, I lie in bed all day. This is when I sing, make up songs to pass the hours, bounce the bedsprings to make them wheeze, same sound as the wheezes in my chest, for in my chest live a frog and a mouse. A frog and a mouse, who like the mattress and me, sing raspy duets.

Days, I come to know, are for easier breathing, nights for terrible feverish heaving. Some nights are so terrible I am unable to cling to the side-hill. All I can do is lie straight back on the slack pillow, both feet braced against my mother's hip, the top of my head close to the cold metal tubes of the bed. Higher, higher I want to lift my head, higher to gasp with open mouth, higher to raise myself beyond the heft of the quilts, higher to strive against the great iron-bar that lies across my chest. Higher, higher. Begging *hai-ya, hai-ya*. Begging and suffering for breath.

These nights, my mother gets up, goes round, bends over me calm. My father gets up, light shining in the hall, saying that even from there he can hear my heart pound. A pounding that is in my ears, in my chest. That trembles the bed. That is stronger than the heft of the quilts, larger than the room of night around me, larger than the small body of my self. Pounding, rhythmic pounding, that makes my head sit up on top clear as a midnight bell.

One night I am struggling so hard my mother calls for my father in the next room to get up. I hear his feet hit the floor with a thud. I know now what will happen. He is getting up and will go downstairs to the kitchen to start the fire.

"I'll be good, I'll be good," I gasp over and over again.

They think I think they are going to punish me. "We're not punishing you, sis."

"We're trying to make you better."

But, they don't know what I mean. I mean, I know what they are going to do for me and I will allow them. I will allow them to steam me. And once the fire is roaring and the water is boiling in the kettle, I will sit obediently under the steam-tent they will rig up by tying a sheet between the hot water tank and one of the kitchen's overhead water pipes.

I will not fight them. I will not struggle. I will sit under the steam-tent in my father's arms. I will not, like I do from bad-tasting medicine, turn my head away. I will bend to the snout of the kettle's brown paper bag. I will put my face into the stinging hot steam and its sickening smell until in my father's arms the iron-bar in my chest gives way.

I will do this willingly, even though my father will say, "No need to struggle, let me hold you," even though his legs through his pyjamas feel uncomfortably hard and his rough hands holding me toward the steam of the brown paper bag needlessly bite into my arms.

I will allow them because I know I will get better: the three of us up together in the middle of the night, wide-awake: my mother of greying hair holding up the corner of the sheet, the blue of her eyes steady, knowing what to do: my father and I in our flannelette pyjamas under the steam-tent wringing wet. The three of us down in the kitchen at four o'clock in the morning, working together, me being good, my mother pouring brown Friar's balsam into the kettle, all of us knowing what to do.

Afterwards, my mother will put me in dry pyjamas warmed on the oven door; my father will carry me upstairs in the same baby blue blanket he brought me down in, blanket that is softly familiar, that protects me from his rough hands, that has a hole. Again I will sleep peacefully in my bed, dry and cool in fresh sheets. Again I will have my arms over the sheet. The room quiet and black and not so cold. The quilts not so heavy. Again I will sleep alone.

One night my mother is bending over me and there is faint light coming into the room from the bulb in the hall. I am face-up and gasping and I tell her I am going to die. I know because my heart does not feel brave. It is jumping, anxiously galloping, its spirit tired. It wants to stop and rest for a long time.

"Mummy, I'm going to die."

"Oh, no, you're not!" Said with absolute force.

"I've seen you worse than this before!"

And she goes back out into the hall, where she is spreading damp sheets on the banister to dry.

I lie gasping. I know this is the worst I have ever been. My mother thinks I am not going to die, but I know I am going to die.

I begin to spin toward the ceiling. I spin through it to the beautiful green and blue country that is on the other side. A place I have visited many times.

As far as I can see, fields of glowing colours of flowers. A place where I walk along a lightly gravelled path until I find a tree to climb, a tree of great leafy branches, high in its trunk a large dark hollow. I crawl into the hollow, go down, down, down, down into its roots, down until I am back in bed, lying on my back, seeing the ceiling above me moving, moving with a weaving motion of powerful muscular snakes, black snakes with yellow spots, yellow snakes with black spots, brilliantly-coloured undulating snakes, snakes above me, snakes within me, boa-constrictor size. I am in the moving and I am seeing the moving at the same time.

Slowly, slowly the vision fades until I am fully awake. I call for my mother, but she is no longer in the hall. She has gone downstairs.

I think to myself, "I did not die."

When she comes upstairs again to see how I am, I tell her where I have been and how the ceiling turned into snakes.

"Don't talk like that!" she says, very upset.

When spring comes, my mother raises the blind halfway, raises the window a crack. Then she comes and sits on the edge of the bed to say goodnight. The room around us is greyish dark, the mirror over the dressing table a round silver glow, the bureau at the foot of the bed and the curve of the bed's rails almost invisible.

"Hear the frogs singing, Maree," my mother says.

I listen, we both listen, to the frogs' voices that are beyond the thin opening of the window, far far out in the cold freshness of the spring night.

> *Peep, peep, water deep*
> *Too cold, can't sleep*

"That's what they're singing," she says, laughing the funny little laugh I am getting to know. Laugh of wanting to tell me something, something she knows is nice, feeling foolish doing so.

"Where are they singing, Mummy?" I ask, happy to have her sitting beside me in the comforting dusky light.

"Down in the deep dark pools by the railroad track," she says.

Long time, we listen.

> *Peep, peep, water deep*
> *Too cold, can't sleep*

So deep the mystery of their voices, so cold the black pools of their homes.

Sometimes in the long summer evenings of being four, if I am not watching the window, I lie in the bed holding onto my toes under the cotton-light of the sheet. I adore my toes, sweet as small pigs.

When I tire of them, I straighten out and lie cool, flailing my arms outside the sheet, flattening down its hem over my chest. Then for awhile, like a baby, I wiggle my hands up before my face. If the light from the setting sun is bright enough, if I hold my fingers close together, I notice, shining through my hands, red light. Hands of red light that amaze me, that are part of me, that are my own.

When I tire of them, I place my arms down again to fold my body into the perfection of the sheet. Then I watch and wait, while the blind dims. I watch and wait for the streamers of light.

Out of the air close to the ceiling they come, streaming toward me like rain toward a windshield, fast-moving tracks of shining drops, streamers of red and green and blue and gold, drops that never quite reach me, disappear, some for a moment lingering a foot or two above the coverings of the bed, single lazy floaters that eventually wink out in the darkening air.

I lie, long time, entranced, trying to keep my eyes open, hoping always to be seeing them. But after awhile, the bed under me gently begins to move, taking me, as if I am floating, to a place behind my head, taking me to dreamland.

Somewhere between four and five, I know not to expect the streamers any more. Their time is over. I know I will not be seeing them again.

I look up at the dusky, pink-striped wallpaper slant, the discoloured plaster square of the ceiling, its bumps and faint lines of cracks my mother wants to cover with maresco. I open, close my eyes hoping I might make the streamers come. They do not come. But I know I will always remember them.

The deer-heads still look down on me from the stripes of the wallpaper border, but their gaze is stiff. I see them. They do not see me.

Second Shift

—age three to four—

It is the time of night under the yellow glow of the kitchen bulb when we see each other.

"She has a great little appetite, but she doesn't grow."

My mother is speaking to a man on the other side of the gleaming white oilcloth, a blond stranger-man who is wearing a white shirt with rolled-up sleeves. Beside him is a black-browed man with a ridged nose, a man whose eyes are cast down on his plate as his fork stabs canned peas. My father. Except at this moment it seems I don't know who he is. It is as though I cannot quite place him. Beside me, my brother, who is digging his sharp sweater-elbow into my side.

Tonight, I am not allowing my mother 'to get something into me'.

"Here, you drop too much."

I do not want her to help. I want to feed my own self, even though my chin is barely at the level of the oilcloth, and my bottom slips on my high stack of cushions. With my own child's curve-handled spoon, I try to scoop supper into my mouth: chopped potato hash, torn-up bacon, canned peas. I do the best I can, even though hash falls from my tipping spoon in greasy bits down my white terry bib, and peas roll away under the table or lie squashed between my brown-ribbed stockinged knees. The bacon, salty and crisp, I get into myself by chewing it from my fingers.

"I am so growing!" I say, looking crossly up at my mother, who stands at the end of the table with the heavy brown teapot from the stove slanting downward in her hand.

I am cross, but as I look up I have another feeling—a feeling I know I will always remember—that I see my mother as though for the first time, a stranger-woman, who has a face of bright blue eyes and long smooth cheeks, topped by browngrey hair that is rolled back from her high forehead into a wreath. I know she makes the wreath with a 'contrivance', a queer yellowish pinching ring. Upstairs, I have climbed up on a chair to pull it down from the high bureau at the end of my bed to try it on my head for a crown. My mother a stranger-woman whose face, as she pours the tea and hands back a green-ribbed cup and saucer to the stranger-man, takes on a look of something that secretly pleases her.

"Your cup," she says.

A look that she keeps tucked into her cheek as she returns the teapot to the warming oven, moves away across the kitchen behind my chair into the night-time pantry to slice more bread, returns with more bread, takes away dishes from the table to the sink, to the pantry again for pieces of apple pie, back and forth, a piece for each of us, mine as big as a grown-up's, me picking the crust apart to get at the syrupy, nutmeg-flavoured pieces of apple, pulling them apart into a mess, to eat all I can of the pie with sticky fingers, the stranger-woman still getting up and down, more tea for the men, more milk for my brother, more milk for me in my enamel cup which I quickly guzzle down, more slices of bread and butter for everyone.

"Will that be all?" she secretly says.

Then, the corner in her cheek gone, she takes the last of the dishes away, comes back with a glum dishcloth that in her red-knuckled hand looks like a dirty-bunched net. Between my brother and me, she reaches down to swipe away crumbs, spills, making the oilcloth gleam fresh and white again, making my brother's elbow disappear, the men to scrape back their chairs, me to stay where I am, settling as far back as I can on the stack of cushions, bracing my feet against the leg of the table to watch my father and the stranger-man make the motions of their cigarettes.

I watch how their thumbnails nick into the blue heads of their matches, set off sputtery flames from the tiny white spots in their nibs; how they stick the cigarettes aslant in their mouths, light their whiskery tips, set them aglow by sucking in their cheeks; how they jut their jaws, twist their lips to send up white puffs of smoke to the cream-painted water pipes of the ceiling, then shake out their matches with flimsy circles of blue smoke that, deep in my nose, smell like dress material from the store that is new and strong and stiff.

I watch their motions of sucking in and blowing out until the cigarettes burn down to stubs and their eyes squint, until the air is so thick with smoke my eyes sting. Motions I watch until the stove cools and the room under the lightbulb grows dim. And my mother at the sink starts banging the pots and pans. Until I sneeze, slide off the cushions to the floor to stand beside my mother at the sink, where I put my head against her leg, suck my thumb, pull insistent on her aproned dress.

*

Tonight this stranger-man is going to sleep in the junkroom upstairs. Because "the day of foxes is over". I know about foxes. I have been to the fox-ranch at the top of the old orchard that, in winter, seen from the icy steps of the back porch, shows through the winter-bare apple trees as an empty wire-encampment.

I have been there, following up the pasture path from the barn in the summer time, my sock feet awkwardly slipping in rubber boots, following after my father and his rubber boots, his carrying of the feeding pail, his every-so-often turnings around to look at me with merry eyes, his free arm reaching back to help me over sharp ridges of pasture rock, smatters of cowdirt, past stinging branches of pale-berried juniper that crowd the path. His merry brown eyes I like. His help, his hand reaching back, I do not want. I want to be climbing by myself. For I am strong and I want to sing my Sunday School song.

> *Jesus loves me, this I know*
> *for the Bible tells me so.*
> *Little ones to him belong,*
> *they are weak, but He is strong.*

I like being strong. I like the way I am climbing. I like the way my clumsy boots are chafing the calves of my legs. I like this wheezy singing of myself, this rising of myself through swiping juniper, cowy freshness, morning dampness, up through friendly scabby rocks.

"I want to climb by my own self!" I complain, rejecting his hand.

"All right, climb by your own self," he says with a laugh, walking faster to see if I can catch up, turning across the pasture slope toward the bluish-slumping wire of the ranch, the wire-gate at its corner, the place where branches of orchard trees poke through the fence.

I know what is coming. When it is time, we will unlatch the gate and noiselessly pass through the magical cut made for us in its mesh. Then, we will walk along laid-down planks through wire corridors, me following my father's boots, keeping my eyes down. Sun on my shoulders, on the top of my head as I clump one loose rubber boot after the other, barely seeing the small grey huts within the wire cages either side. Once, twice, daring to look up through the fascination of the mesh to see deep blue sky, noticing, as my eyes come down to follow the planks, that it is as though we are walking under grey cloud, walking until we come to the last cage door, my father opening it to throw meat from the pail into the cage, while I stand and wait for the fox to come out of his long wooden-burrow, knowing as I look in at the pen's flat ground, its worn corners of worried grass and mud and turds, not to put my fingers through the holes in the wire, to keep them to myself.

First the nose, the dark pointed head of sharp ears, then the lank darkgrey body, the drawing out into the open of the bushy white-tipped tail, an animal slinky and furtive—not at at all like our small Trixie-dog when she wedges out from under the kitchen stove—an animal that does not see us, cannot see us, because it seems to me it has no eyes.

"I know what is going to happen to you," I soundlessly whisper from a sunken place I feel on my insides.

I know that the animal gulping down its feed on the far side of the cage is going to be changed into a flat crackling skin, turned inside out and stretched on a pointed board, its head flattened out and three-cornered holes made for its lost eyes, the board to be propped against the wall of the junk-room upstairs for the skin to dry. The animal is going to be a pelt, a drying crackling pelt with a great tail of soft fur hanging down softer than my cheek.

"Why?" I have asked my father.

"We can't make pets of them," he says.

*

My mother and father and Harold and I go up to the junk-room to make room for the stranger-man's bed, all of us together in its icy cold, its foxy smell, a smell that is sharper than earwax, stronger than dog. The four of us, up here strangely, it seems, after chores, together inside the hidden room around the corner at the top of the stairs, behind its white-painted door where Harold and I are normally not allowed. The four of us. Milling around under the clear bulb that shows the glowing filament inside. Up here to clear the room, set up a bed. Stranger-man sitting downstairs. Already dark night in the window outside.

"I'll never get the smell out!" my mother says.

With enthusiasm my mother and father set to work, take the last of the fox pelts off the stretch-boards, carry them out of the room, lay them down tattery on the hall floor, their soft bushy tails mixing with the rungs of the stairs' railing, next bringing out the stretch-boards to stand like staves against the wall at the top of the stairs.

"Now you stay out of the way, Maree."

"Harold, you can do this," my father says, lifting him so my mother can hand him the stretch-boards to jab one by one up through the black attic hole just outside the junk-room door.

"Far as you can reach, son, far as you can reach."

Going back into the room, my father with my mother's help clangs together a bed from iron frames, an old spring, a slumping mattress that lean against the east wall, me hopping and skipping about, Harold helping to lift the supporting iron rails from the floor. A bed for the stranger-man, where he will sleep.

"I can't wait to paper everything over," my mother says, on her way out of the room to see if she can find clean sheets. "When some money comes in."

She is going to cover over gloomy holes in the walls that show whole sections of grey lathes, holes that have webs hanging in them, quivering with crumbles. That I am not to touch. Because already I am sneezing. With the foxsmell in the cold air is a smell that is like the smell of the cubbyhole downstairs, a smell that is beginning to cut like wire into my chest, burn my eyes, turn my nose into a long sticky burning drip.

"Go out of here, Maree, we have to sweep," my mother says.

"Go out and wait in the hall," my father says.

I don't want to wait in the hall.

"She never does what she's told," my brother says.

"I want to stay!"

There is something I have spied, something with my little eye, under the eave at the back of the room, a tall cardboard box. I want to see it, crawl into it, pull everything out that is in it, no matter that I am sneezing, wheezing and getting short of breath.

"I want to see what's in it!" I cry, pulling up the box's flaps, diving over its wobbly side to pull out messes of clothes, musty-knitted sweaters with holes in the elbows, wrinkled chilly-feeling crepe dresses, tough trouser pants, smashed flowered hats.

"Those old crepe dresses!" my mother exclaims, stopping to look at the things I have dragged onto the floor.

"Throw them out, for godssakes, missus."

"Some of them are Helen's," my mother says.

"Helen be damned," my father says.

With the brooms from the kitchen and the porch—Harold helping by holding the dustpan—they sweep the dust out from under the set-up bed, work to clear crumbles of plaster and cobwebby flies scattered under the window and along the baseboards. I stay where I am, pulling dresses up around me like I have seen my mother do, one cherryred, one navyblue, holding them against me and my raspy breathing, pulling them up to my chin, up to my face to wipe their cubbyhole smell against my dripping nose.

*

The stranger-man is an Englishman out of the war. In a day or two when it is suppertime again under the dim yellow bulb, he will hold me on his lap before he goes out to help with the chores. He will tell me that I will be a heart-smasher when I grow up. And I will watch his blue eyes which have a slant. And his moving mouth. I will listen to his voice, which has a pleasant sound when he talks, like the sound the stove makes when it burns fresh dry wood.

After the Englishman and my father have gone to the barn to milk the cows, my mother repeats what he has said to me, as if I were a grown-up:

"He thinks you'll be a heart-smasher when you grow up," she says, pleased, very pleased.

I know she is pleased, very pleased, because she laughs the same little laugh she laughs when she is standing at the stove frying pale rings of doughnuts, same laugh she laughs when she is lifting them up with the slotted spoon, a nice rich brown colour out of the bubbling hot lard, round and crusted.

"They're going to be good, if I do say so myself!" is what she says.

O I am glad I'm going to be a heart-smasher when I grow up.

I like to sit on the Englishman's lap, I like the feel of his cotton shirt with the sleeves rolled up, the furry feel of the golden hair on his arms. I laugh and carry on, beg gleefully for his attention. He laughs, and jostles me, and his arms care to hold me. And he tells me I have beautiful black eyes. I am a heart-smasher. Now!

A few days more and I will hear my mother and father say, when the Englishman is outside in the yard, that as far as they can make out he is a sailor who must have jumped ship. My mother saying, that while she does not want a hired man around, "he's a better type than some you might get." And my father saying that while he may be clean and polite enough to suit her, "he's none too swift around the barn," and it is like an Englishman to think he knows it all.

"You can't tell them anything," he says.

A few days more, maybe a week, out from under the lightbulb he is gone. Because when he is working in the barn, a hook from a pulley in the milkroom draws back and stabs him in the eye. And he has to go to the doctor. And he has to wear a white patch. And he has to go back somewhere on the main road to the east that is far beyond the winter darkness, the house and the road we live on.

"We didn't need a hired man anyway," my mother says.

Yes, we do need a hired man.

"If I'm going to milk more cows," my father says.

Another hired man comes, not from jumping off a ship, but from down Meteghan way. A hired man who has a name, and smells like his name, Malcolm, heavy and thick. A Malcolm who sits on the other side of the gleam of the oil-cloth, eyes down, who bends into his food, who when he drinks his glass of milk dampens with dribbles the corners of his fleshy lips. My mother says she cannot stand this. His slop and drip. My father, eyes darting angry flashes, says Malcolm is as strong as an ox, if my mother wants to know.

Some nights, Malcolm keeps house. And my brother and I are upstairs with Malcolm tumbling around on Harold's bed, getting the bedding all stirred up, trying not to hit our heads on the ceiling slope, giggling after things that are hidden under the top quilt, a hand, a foot, a comic book.

One of these things is Malcolm's dink. The thing of boys girls are not supposed to see, say anything about or know. Me diving around, standing up, wallowing in my long nightgown over the rumpled bed, Harold every so often yanking me up by the feet to steer me like a wheel-barrow over Malcolm's thick chest, his heavy restless legs, steering me wiggling and screaming until I fall face down in the soft snuffling blackness of the quilt.

Why can't I see?

Why is it not nice to see? I have seen a boy's thing. I have seen Harold pee.

We carry on, high glee, the boys laughing and wrestling, me barking and jumping and squealing, pretending that I am like Trixie when out by the woodpile she digs a hole, wallowing and digging, until I start to cough.

"You ca-an't see-ee," Harold taunts.

"I ca-an so-o."

I can see. When Malcolm gets out from under the quilt to go to his room, ready for bed in his saggy underwear top and shorts, I can sort of see his thing, something pinkish peeping through a divide in the cloth.

"Go to bed you two," he thickly says.

But Harold and I go on wrestling. Because I can do anything he can do.

I can be just as strong, even though he can hold me down, sit on me, wrench my arms, make me cry. I can be just as strong, because I do not give up, I will not give up. I bite, pinch, scratch. He is stronger, but I am fiercer. I know this sure as sure. Even though I am gasping for breath and my arms are growing weak and my face is oven-hot.

"We'll see who's stronger," Harold says, suddenly trapping my thrashing legs between his tough knees and reaching for a bed pillow to thump it down over my face.

"Let me go! let me go!" I cry, trying to breathe through the pillow's suffocating weight.

But the more I cry, the more he bears down. So that my mouth can make no sound at all, can only move wetly against the pillow's threads. I strain with all my might, but nothing I can do moves his body off. His elbows like spades dig into my arms, his hands bear down harder, thicken the pillow's suffocation over my face.

"Give up! give up!"

I strain more. Panicking. Lungs bursting. Heart pounding. Without air I will die. I will die here under the heft of the pillow's darkness with a strange feeling of lightness swimming in my head. But I know what to do. I will pretend. I will go limp. Go limp until he thinks I am dead, go limp until (if I do not die) I will feel his body give, resentfully throw the pillow aside.

I go limp until, with terrible gasping, shuddering sobs, I am dazedly looking up into the slanted ceiling's yellowish glare.

"That'll teach you, that'll teach you!" my brother taunts some more, going out of the room into Malcolm's room.

Teach me, teach me to give up?

I'll never give up.

"I won't, I won't!" I sob.

"Go to bed and shut up!"

*

Malcolm does not stay long. He is homesick. Someone else comes up from some place down Digby way. His name is funny, but not so thick. His name is Hershel, strange and rustling like a dark branch. In the spring sunlight he wears a faded plaid shirt. In the kitchen he smells of sour sweat. He keeps the door to his room shut. He stays for the summer to help hay. My father wants him to stay on.

"I need a man permanent," he says.

"We can pick our own apples," my mother says.

"We don't need anyone for the winter. What would we do with him?"

"Haul wood, help with the cows."

"I'm tired and sick of looking after a hired man," my mother says.

Late summer, my mother decides to board the new school teacher instead. A tall pleasant woman who is a whiz at double solitaire, who, my mother says, has beautifully manicured hands, who knits beautifully, too, who goes home on Friday nights. Whose name is Maxine MacBride.

My mother gives her Harold's room, because the junk room with its bigger iron bed "is not good enough", even though they have repaired the gloomy broken places in the wall and thrown the old sagging mattress over the dump and replaced it with one from Aunt Frances' spare bedroom.

I go into Harold's room with my mother to get things ready, to help her, by standing under the eave, to pull away the heavy black quilt, the sheets that cover the three-quarter bed, so she can drape a clean flannelette sheet over the mousey-smelling mattress, tuck around it fresh, white, off-the-line sheets, spread over them a pale patchwork quilt, float over it the lightness of a white cotton bedspread taken from her own bed. The bedspread is very pretty; its oval centre has tiny daisy flowers stitched with pink and blue and yellow embroidery thread.

A day or so later we go into the room and take the bedding off again, even the mattress, take everything off down to the harsh metal net of the bed's spring, remove the brass knobs at the corners of its frame, and with my father helping, take the whole bed apart, up-ending the spring against the slant of the wall.

Saying, "I'll do it," in an annoyed voice, he carries the headboard and footboard out into the hall, where my mother, after putting down newspapers, takes a paint brush and laps strong-smelling white paint over the frame's chipped metal curves. This time I help by staying away from her work, by not always asking to be doing things.

She is not able right now, she says, to re-paper the walls of Maxine's room, only to replace the window's darkgreen ripped blind with a cream one from the catalogue, "like the one in your room".

"It turns orange," I say.

"How I detest those old dark green blinds of Mumma's," she says.

"How long's before Maxine MacBride coming?" I ask, hoping tomorrow.

"Two weeks. When it's time for school."

One morning, after making the beds and before we go downstairs, my mother and I stop at the threshold of Harold's old room to see how the room looks finished. I put my hand up to take hers while we observe the prettiness of everything, the white bedstead with its dainty curves, the white spread that flows down over its side to just touch the blue linoleum of the floor, the pretty oval of the tiny pink and blue and yellow flowers at its centre that looks like a shy garden, and the newly polished brass knobs at three of the frame's four corners which seem to glow like guardians. The one missing, my mother says, may never be found.

"Perhaps it's just as well."

Because if it were there, it might gouge a hole in the ceiling slope of the wall if the bed got jarred.

I squeeze my mother's fingers. I like to hold her fingers, even if they do have the damp feeling of after doing dishes. My mother is pleased that the room is pretty. I am pleased she is pleased. Opposite us, the morning sun shines under the edge of the new cream blind, lights up yellow the ruffles of the priscilla curtains.

"It's pretty," I say softly.

"At least it's clean," my mother says.

There is more to do, always more to do, before the coming of Maxine MacBride. Another bedspread is ordered from the catalogue to replace the bedspread taken from my parents' room for Maxine's bed, a white, too-thin chenille which my mother decides not to bother sending back.

"For our room it will do."

To make a better room for Harold, the tattered square of yellow-brown linoleum on the junk room floor, also from Aunt Francis, is shuffled away and replaced by a larger, oily-smelling square from Roops that has a 'mottled-green effect'. Also, my mother says, she is thinking of covering the old black wool quilt which in Harold's new room now serves as a bedspread for the bigger iron bed. Maybe she can make it look like something, she says. But this she does not do.

"That old black quilt of Mumma's. But it's warm."

An old black and brown quilt that I like to crawl around on, because it feels deep and dark and warm to my nudging knees, not like the other quilts in the house with their dry puckered surfaces that feel cool. Its soft black and brown wool patches my mother says are cut out of old worn-out wool suits, trousers, coats, cast-off clothes.

"They used up everything years ago."

"Mumma always was one for saving," my mother says.

Mumma is my mother's mother. Grandmother Barrett. A tall large-bodied woman who lives up east. A woman who stays in her bedroom off the kitchen at Uncle Spencer's, who comes out sometimes into the dining room to eat macaroni and cheese. Who has long black hair that, when it is taken down out of the bun at the back of her neck, falls below her waist. Grandmother Barrett who speaks to my mother only a little. Who does not say anything to me.

*

Maxine finally comes. A woman so tall I can barely see her.

"You'd hardly know she's here," my mother says.

Sometimes, though, I see her on a winter evening when the fire in the living room's black stove is lit and I am sitting on the sofa. I look up and see her, split-second, in the brown velour chair under the pleated yellow glow of the bridge lamp, reading a book. A lamp that is hooked up by a long brown twisty cord to a round white plug on the wall behind the chair that I am never to touch. Unless I want to be electrocuted.

Sometimes, I see her for longer when I am lying quiet under a blanket on the sofa, wheezing in my damp pyjamas. I see her in a darkgreen sweater and a green-and-black plaid skirt spreading down over her long lyle-stockinged legs that stretch toward the red glowing teeth of the stove's grate, her feet in black fur-trimmed slippers crossed at the ankles.

Mostly, though, I see her in the kitchen sitting at the end of the table next to the white frost of the north window, sometimes playing solitaire, sometimes knitting. I see her shuffle cards, arrange, re-arrange them on the table, red and black layers of diamonds, spades, hearts, clubs, aces, ornamental faces of jacks, queens, kings.

Especially I like to watch her knit, see the way her long smooth fingers like pink-polished steeples dart forward, loop the yarn again and again over the needle's sharp point, see how her other hand grips the needle that has falling from it a panel of soft floppy pink sweater, see how she deftly shifts along the loops of wool.

Sometimes I stand close enough to peek up into her placid heart-shaped face, her dark blue eyes gazing down, see how her rosy-lipsticked mouth moves to speak to my mother standing against the warm oven-door of the stove.

"I'm too vain to smile," my mother says.

"You look just fine, smile anyway," Maxine says.

In my mother's mouth, I have noticed a mixture of gold and white and silver teeth.

"You start losing teeth when you have kids, Ray has trouble with his teeth, too," my mother says.

"Too much sweet," Maxine says.

In my father's mouth are teeth with wires, and a gap back inside his mouth that shows a silver hook when he smiles.

"I tell Ray he looks like Mahatma Gandhi," my mother says with her secret cheek-smile.

"You make me laugh!" Maxine says.

"Who's Mahatma Gandhi?" I ask, wondering at the funny name.

"A man from India," my mother says.

She says his picture is in the paper.

I want to see it, I want to see what funny name my father looks like. I dance around to insist. But my mother says she used that paper to start the morning fire.

*

Friday nights, excitement. Maxine's boyfriend Reg comes to pick her up, to take her to a movie, to take her home to West Pleasant Valley, to take her to her parents' place for the week-end. Friday nights, Reg in the kitchen, in the wood chair that he lifts out to the centre of the kitchen from beside the stove's grate. Reg, whose tanned face looks sharp as a fox, whose black hair is combed back damp and straight with sweet-smelling hair oil, who has good teeth.

"Thank goodness," my mother says.

Reg who laughs, likes to play wrestle-arm games with Harold, lets me perch on his wavering knee while my father just in from the barn (my mother at the sink finishing things) settles in a chair by the table, his eyes twinkling, smiling his Mahatma Gandhi smile.

All of us together joking and teasing and playing, waiting for Maxine, listening for her steps tapping down the stairs, hearing her come along the hall, waiting to see her stoop through the door, tall Maxine in her slim dark brown skirt and loafers, her rosy angora sweater and string of pearls, her lightbrown hair in clumps about her ears, her face lit up with a ceiling-smile, her dimming of the kitchen bulb as she lowers herself to sit on Reg's other knee, all of us laughing because it is easy to see that I am very small and she is very big.

Janet Parker Vaughan

Third Shift

—age three to four—

The air of the bedroom is black, so black it shines. The door to the upstairs hall is shut. Outside, winter-night. Snow on the ground. On the window, frost.

My brother and I lie awake, side by side under quilts, put in bed together this once and only time of our lives. Above us, unseeable, the ceiling slant. Beyond it, black starless sky. Behind my pillow, in the northeast, rising on a slow curve over the dark ridge of the mountain and its snowy trees, Santa. Santa coming in his beauty-red sleigh with eight brown reindeer, Santa slowly sailing over the bare-branched orchard, the dark frozen hollow until clearly I hear, O so clearly, the soft jingle of bells, the slip and crunch of runners, the tapping hooves of reindeer on the roof.

"I hear him," I whisper to Harold.

"You can?" he says, believing me.

We listen together, shushing each other, listen for sounds of Santa coming down the central chimney in the upstairs hall.

"He won't come if we don't sleep," I say.

What our parents say.

"Then close your eyes," my brother says.

Together we sense the darkness of the room, the frost on the window, the snugness of the house, the cold of the snow outside. On the mountain, shining winged-angels stand among snow-covered trees. Below them in the barn, in the dark warm stable, cattle lowing, a baby is born whose name is Jesus Christ. Under the shared weight of the quilts, my brother and I dream deep in golden light.

The next morning we run downstairs lickety-split, our parents trailing behind us. We burst through the door from the icy hall into the lukewarm living room. There in a dusky corner is a dark green tree. Its boughs, which smell of wet woods, are hung with soft faded red rope, with ornaments of small metallic cones that in the faint bulb-light from the hall shine gold and blue and green.

Beneath the boughs are bundles of presents wrapped in dull red and green tissue paper. Among them, unwrapped, are the presents Santa has left: a doll for me; for Harold a puck and hockey stick.

The doll has a plain blue polka dot dress and stubby cloth legs, a colourless cloth face on which is painted a red mouth, black dots for a nose, blue spots for eyes. Not the doll I wanted. Not a real doll with a real face of blue eyes and brown lashes and pretty brown curls, who wears a pretty pink lace-trimmed dress, not like the doll I have seen in the catalogue.

I pick her up and hold her, stiff homely thing, against my chest.

"You don't like your doll, sis?" my father says from the hall doorway.

"Looks like Santa didn't have the doll you wanted," my mother says, coming in to stand beside me.

Then she points. "Why, my goodness, he's pinned a note to the back of her skirt!"

The note says, my mother reading it, that Santa did not have enough money for a doll like the one in the catalogue, maybe next year. I know, with a feeling that digs on the inside of me, that my mother has written this note and that Santa Claus did not write it at all.

I pretend to like the doll. The homely doll will feel bad if I don't hold her close to myself.

*

Not while the war is on.
While the war is on, we have to make do.
If the war ends soon...

I stare through the glinty-black cloth that hangs behind the radio's slatted face. Deep inside I see a tiny orange coal of light. The war is in there, encased in that tiny coal of light. I stare at it, hearing through oceanic static what sound like barking voices, voices, my mother tells me, that come to us because of tubes. Tubes inside the radio that pick up signals out of the air from far away and bring them here.

"I want you to remember that's Churchill. He is fighting Hitler," my mother says.

Hitler is a wicked dictator who wants to take over the world. Churchill is a great man who will not let him. I know about soldiers and tanks and aeroplanes and bombs and how armies face each other and shoot guns to see who can shoot down dead the most men and win. I know this from the lead soldiers my brother sets up on the kitchen floor and the small metal Spitfire aeroplanes he flies over the soldiers to shoot them down with bullets and bombs "kerpow" to get rid of them. But, here, this side of the glinty-black cloth of the screen we are safe.

So I am told, but this I do not wholly believe. Because as I listen and stare through the curtain, sometimes the tiny orange light inside the radio seems to expand into a place that is called overseas and there I can see Hitler advancing, not a man with a mustache, but an ironblack engine of terrible revolving wheels that flattens everything in its track, that rolls over people trying to shoot at it with little guns, that crushes them into the mud. This frightens me because it seems that faraway might become here.

But my mother says the war is on the other side of the water, the Atlantic Ocean. "Don't worry, Hitler can't come here."

Hitler can't come here. But down the road is Hitler's old friend, a man whose name is Otto Strasser. He is a man who has escaped the machine of Hitler, and he lives in the house on a farm my father rents. He lives with his secretary Margarita and some other people, people who have white blonde hair who are called Czechs.

Margarita is nice. She is from Spain, a woman with upswept goldenbrown hair. She is the one who helped Otto escape from the machine by dressing herself up like a boy; she is the one who got him across the Atlantic Ocean on a boat to here, where it is safe.

"Hitler even killed his friends," I hear my father say.

"Why?" I ask.

"Because they wouldn't do what he wanted them to do."

"What does he want them to do?"

"Think like him," my father says.

My mother and father talk a lot about Otto and Margarita, especially when people drive in the yard and come into the kitchen to visit, people like Gladstone Potter and Aubrey Hicks, relatives like Uncle Spencer and Aunt Edna from Kings County where my parents, when they were a boy and girl, like my brother and me growing up here in Annapolis County, used to live.

I am curious to hear everything they say, because I know Otto and Margarita are very different from us. I like it that they are different. I like to listen to the talk of my parents and Gladstone Potter and Aubrey Hicks.

Otto, I hear, is a very smart man, but he does not understand how it is that if there is a drought in Halifax we can still have water here in Wilmot running out of the taps. Margarita, I hear, is also smart.

"I think she's a little more than a secretary, myself," Gladstone Potter says, with a wink.

Gladstone Potter is a saucy man from up the road. He has a funny knobbly bald head.

"I like Margarita, all the same," my mother says.

"So do I," I say, making them laugh.

Margarita is smart because she can speak and read and write in five languages. I seem to grasp what a language is: a language is when someone speaks entirely different words for words in your own language that mean the same thing. Margarita's name in Spanish and my mother's name in English, Margaret, are really the same name. Although my mother says she is not sure, but that Margarita might have started out French. But then her name would be Marguerite.

Margarita sits most days at a typewriter and translates what Otto writes in German, the language that comes out of his mouth, into the language that comes out of our mouths, English. There are many different languages overseas, I am told, because there are many different countries.

Once upon a time in a faraway country...

A country is like a place in a story, way out beyond the edge of your mind. A country is a faraway land where fields and roads and houses and woods and brooks go on and on farther and farther than driving from Annapolis County to Kings County. To go to another country, you have to cross water or a border, like when people go to the States. To cross a border is like crossing a county line. A border is like when you see a sign like the sign my mother points to when on Sunday afternoons—if we have enough gas—we get in the truck and cross into Kings County over the Annapolis County line. Then, it's like we are in another country that we sometimes call Up East: the place where Grandmother Barrett and Grammie Grave, Uncle Spencer and Aunt Edna and Aunt Frances and Aunt Muriel and all kinds of relatives, aunts and uncles and cousins live. There the language is almost the same, except Uncle Spencer says things like "And all that kind of biz." I do not know what biz is.

Some evenings my father goes to visit Otto down at the 'other place' in a room that has a bare wood floor. I have been in this room myself, because some mornings my mother sends me down to the 'other place' with my father in the truck. Unlike our living room of brown velvet sofa and matching curved stuffed chairs, where I crawl up from the swishy blue leaves of the linoleum floor to be cosy, Otto and Margarita's living room seems made of sticks.

Along the room's sides, placed against its varnished baseboards, are thin-legged chairs, a thin-legged desk, a thin-legged book case, and thin-legged tables, on which sit heavy wooden radios that have peaked heads like churches and ugly faces of nobs and dials.

Radios that are not a bit like our big cabinet radio at home that stands straight up strong from the floor on feet that look like huge claws.

Around the walls, looking like dirty clouds, are tacked large maps. With these maps, marked all over in red and black ink, my father says Otto 'follows the war' and always knows what Hitler is going to do next.

The maps, my father says, show the roads and rivers and borders of Europe. And I know what a map is. It is the same thing as when Harold and I take sticks and shape pictures of hills and brooks and roads and fences and houses and barns in the gravel heap outside the garage.

Whenever I visit, Otto looks down at me from under enormous bushy eyebrows and greets me in a jolly manner. He does this because I am a child. His way of saying hello is very different from, say, Aubrey Hicks, who comes in the house and sits straddling a chair with his felt hat on, and who does not say anything to me or look at me at all. Otto's way of saying hello is to bend over and take my hand as if to kiss it. I am pleased Otto pays this attention to me.

Once he was Hitler's friend, but not now, so I am not afraid of him. I am not afraid of him or Margarita, or of the white-blond, broad-faced Czech people they live with. But I am made shy by them. By their language I do not understand. By Otto's voice that rolls explosively out of his chest. By the way, whenever we drive in his yard to deliver vegetables or a message, he rushes out the back door to meet us. Then, I stand close to my father's leg. If we go in the house to visit for a few minutes, I crawl up on my father's lap.

"Smart man," my father says. "But I wouldn't trust him."

"He could just as easily be a dictator, too," my father says.

"He'd be just as bad as Hitler when it comes to the Jews."

I will soon know about Jews because of the day Cora Henderson, who is looking after two little boys called DPs, gets sick with flu. She calls my mother and asks her to help by setting up two cribs for them in our living room. Twin Jewish boys 'displaced' from France, who are named Peter and Paul. They cry and want to nap together using only one crib, so I have my afternoon nap beside them, my mother letting me crawl into the unused one, where I watch them between the bars. Two little boys with dark hair and matching white faces and black eyes that stare back.

"Their heads are perfectly shaped," my mother says.

My head I understand is not perfectly shaped because my mother says to my father that my head is flat at the back "like yours".

"But her hair will cover it," she says.

The twins stay only a day or two until my mother gets sick and Cora is well enough to take them back.

"They are going to be sent to Montreal."

"Where's their mother?" I ask.

"Probably dead," my mother says. "Their father, too."

Hitler wanted to kill the Jews, wanted to see them dead, wanted to get rid of them.

"Does Otto want to see them dead?" I ask, thinking he might go to this Montreal place to get rid of Peter and Paul.

"Oh, I don't think he'd go that far."

"Why did Hitler want to see them dead?"

The mother and father of Peter and Paul.

But my mother does not want to answer any more questions, she wants to close her eyes and rest because having the twins "along with everything else" has made her very tired.

"It seems I am only able to look after my own," she says.

One Saturday my mother, who is going to Institute in Annapolis where she is going to make a speech, asks Margarita to come and keep house for us kids.

"Won't you stay for supper, Margarita?" she asks.

Margarita says "yes" and hopes it will not be any trouble. It will not be trouble because my mother already knows what we are going to eat. She has something she is going to make when she gets home that will come out of a package.

"Sorry, it won't be Boston brown bread and beans," my mother says to Margarita, as she goes out the door to get in the car of Mrs. Wilhelmina Rumsey, a woman with a straight black straw hat who is glad to give her a ride.

My brother and I like Margarita, and she likes my brother and me, especially Harold, whom she calls Hahld, who behaves for her, who, when she comes to keep the house, behaves nicer to me. This seems to have something to do with the way Margarita sounds to us, the way her accented voice has a hollow in it that sounds goldendark, the way she feels to us, as if she wore a coat of firm goldendark cloth.

Today, while our mother is away, we are going in the cab on a trip to Centreville, where my father is taking a truckload of apples to have ground into pomace, Harold sitting in the middle with his legs around the gear, I on Margarita's lap, her arms around me like my mother's when she holds me, but not as closely, not the way my mother holds me so I blend into her lap,

Margarita's arms around me feeling more like a sheltering protection from the jolts of the rutted roads.

Both my brother and I know something about Margarita she does not know we know. She has children. She has children somewhere overseas in one of the dirty cloud map-countries on Otto's wall. Two little girls. But we are never to ask.

"Who knows whether she will see them again," my mother tells my brother and me. "Who knows if they are alive."

If they are alive, maybe they do not know their mother is here in far-off Annapolis County safe from Hitler, far off across the Atlantic Ocean in this cab of a truck going to Centreville to grind apples for pomace, their mother here holding me.

"They may think she is dead, too," my mother says.

I look around at Margarita and watch her face gazing out the window.

I wonder if she is sad holding me.

When we get home and my mother gets home, we open up the door of the cool-feeling dining room to let the warmth of the kitchen in. Only on company nights do we get to eat there, me on two cushions on the brown leather-seated chair, bending carefully over the white tablecloth that has a wide gold band like wallpaper border running around its hem.

Tonight I get to use a long silver spoon that my mother takes out of the green-lined box in the buffet. Tonight, with Margarita here, my mother lifts me up to see the box deep down in the buffet's top

48

drawer, so I can see the shining knives, forks and spoons in the box's compartments, very neat.

"They aren't that good, they're only plate," she says.

Beneath the box my mother has something stored.

"Something for you kids."

"Something I want you to know about in case I die," she says.

"War Bonds."

When we are ready to eat, the four of us, with Margarita for company, sit around the square table under the round shell of the pale dining room light, my father at the south-end, his dark face lit up with smiling, Margarita on the west side of the table hunched a little, smiling too, her head, with all the goldendark hair up top, nodding, Harold and I on the east side with elbows touching, him-me, me-him, my mother at the head of the table with a flushed face serving our plates with sloppy spoonfuls from a casserole dish of soft slippery tomatoey noodles.

"This spaghetti can't be like the spaghetti you have at home, can it Margarita?" my mother says.

To which Margarita, taking a sip, replies, "No, ours ees spice."

To me the soft slippery noodles taste sickish, have a nasty orangey blood-coloured taste. I look over at Margarita gently dipping at the plate with her fork. Her face from its pleasant nodding has gone plain. I know she does not like this spaghetti; it is not what she has at home in Spain.

To make it taste better, I stuff into my mouth with every spoonful a small piece of buttered bread, wash the works down with large swallows of milk. Margarita also takes a slice of bread and without any swallows of milk does the same.

We hear Margarita tell my mother that Harold and I are bright. And after my father takes Margarita home in the truck, my mother says it over again to us, as she stands putting away dishes in the pantry.

"She thinks you kids are bright."

I can tell this pleases our mother very much. Because out of her blue eyes beams a light that helps her see far out through the panes of the pantry window at least halfway as far as Palmers'.

I know what bright is. It is a clear feeling I get when I can see overseas expand inside the radio from its tiny coal light, when I know what is meant when my mother has something "to explain". Bright is clear. Not like the shadowy yellow kitchen bulb when someone big is standing in the way. Bright is knowing what bright is. Bright is like dancing on tiptoe over the lawn on a clear sunny day.

Bright is counting up to ten, then twenty, thirty, forty, fifty; saying abcdefg; recognizing words off the Rice Krispie box, snap crackle pop; learning with small stubborn fingers how to shell peas. Bright is catching on quickly, quickly, like the little gasp of air I take before telling my mother the right answer when she points to a word in the Ing family of names I have printed in chalk on the small blackboard that sits on the windowseat upstairs. Bright is being quick, causes grown-ups 'to make of you'. A bit like being a heart smasher.

Fourth Shift

—age three to four—

I have a question. A question I have had inside myself for some time. It is a question that is like a feeling. I am sitting near the stove in the kitchen, sitting on a patch of worn brown linoleum in the way I feel most comfortable, one bare leg straight out, the other one bent behind me. All around me are strewn stubby wheels of faded colours and thin wooden sticks, also strawberry boxes of red-stained pale wood, some loose and set out individually, some still jammed together in tipped-over towers fallen as far as under the kitchen table.

It is the time of evening just before supper when the kitchen is cosywarm and smells of pork fat. The time when my mother stands at the stove with a pancake turner, poking and scraping at potato and onion in a black frying pan.

It is a feeling that I have landed out of nowhere to sit upright here and I do not know why. I have landed, and I am looking up at a woman in a faded pink dress, who is cooking over a silver-decorated black stove. To the left of her is a tall water tank that has thin pale slack things hanging down from its pipes that look like diapers.

I have this feeling and it makes a question in my head. Where have I come from if this is where I am, sitting on a floor behind a woman with stoutish legs clad in brown stockings, with feet in beaded wine-coloured slippers, one foot toed-in, the other pointed into the under-stove darkness? A toed-in foot that has a thick ankle.

Why am I here?

Why here, sitting among stubby wheels and sticks and strawberry boxes on a smooth brown floor that holds me up, as though to keep me from falling through to some unknown other side. A feeling and a thought, queer and familiar at the same time.

*

This time, with the feeling on me, I ask, "How come I'm here?"

My mother turns around from the stove. She does not hesitate.

"The stork brought you to the hospital."

I do not expect this kind of answer. A stork? What is a stork, a word that has an amusing sound. A funny sort of cart with a short hitching pole? Like the one stored on the other side of the black jinglebell sleigh I have seen in the old horse barn?

I ask again, looking up to my mother who no longer has a pancake turner in her hand, but the metal mustard can that is the hash-chopper. "Where do I come from?"

Before here.

"Nobody knows where anybody comes from," she says, her voice almost in a whisper. "We're just here."

But I know that somehow I have come out of the air. Somewhere behind the watertank. And I have mysteriously settled here in this body of head, arms, stomach, upright back, one leg straight out, one leg bent in behind. I am somewhere before I am here sitting in this darkened yellow kitchen looking out through my eyes. Somewhere. But I cannot remember where. Somewhere where there is not a smell of pork fat in the air.

"Why don't we know?" I ask.

*

I am too little to see out, but outside the cab I am aware of grey trunks of trees glimming by, of white fronts of verandahed houses, of lawns that slide out of sight behind us leaving inside the open cab window their sneezy smell of fresh cut grass. Above, where I can see, light shimmies down the slimness of overhanging limbs like rain falling toward the windshield glass.

I am going into town with my father, who drives with resigned hands on the wheel, the peak of his tan cap drawn down over his black brows. My father, who does not want me here.

I am only here going into town because my mother at home in a grey-shingled house on a road under a mountain wants to get things done, and I have acted up and cried. Why I am now being good. Why the lawns and trees and houses are sliding away and the light from on high through the glass is providing shy warmth for my brown-ribbed knees, why there is a great sound of bells dinging and donging over the engine's monotonous grind.

"Bells," I say.

"All the bells of the churches are ringing at once," my father says.

"Why?"

I know it is not Sunday.

"Because the war is over. Hitler's finished, he's gone."

My father lifts his cap to set the peak straight out from his forehead, his brown eyes shooting sudden happy light over to my side.

Hitler gone.

Hitler and his terrible machine gone, gone.

"All the soldiers overseas are coming home," my father says.

"Hitler gone, gone. Hitler, Hitler gone, gone. . ," the bells wildly, recklessly, happily ring as our truck turns the corner at the centre of town, chugs up the street to the long grey warehouses alongside the railroad track next to Nixon's mill.

"Guess they aren't open," my father says, jolting to a halt.

No other trucks around. Everything quiet.

"But we'll go and see anyway," my father says, turning off the engine, jumping out of the cab to come around to my side, to help me slide to the muddy grooves of the running board, so from there I can jump free in my rubber boots to the mud-puddled ground.

"Gon...ne...gonne...gone...gonne...gone.ne.ong.ong.ong..." the bells ring back in the centre of town.

We stand listening, my father and I, looking back the way we have come, the empty curving street with its tall leafless trees of spring, the white boxes of houses with their small green lawns.

"Gon...ne...gonne...ong.ong."

We stand listening, my small hand in his rough hand. Me, feeling sad in the hollow of my throat, in my sore chest that slightly wheezes, in my belly that swells under my long droopy coat, sad down my legs to where my rubber boots cut into my calves, sad right down to my toes.

We turn to walk toward the lumber office that might be open, might be, maybe...not, because today the war is over and everybody is home and there is no commotion of rumbling trucks, no piercing wail of saws. All in the lumberyard is still. There are only the silent peaks of the yard's huge piles of slab.

*

It is almost noon, and the turnip is slow to cook and my mother is showing me how to tell time.

"I want to turn the hands," I say from the floor, scrambling up.

"I'll show you," she says.

Raising the clock above my head so I can see it, but not reach it, working the key at its back to whirl the slim arrows of the hands around and around the black numbers on the dial, she shows me on-the-hour, half-hour, quarter-to, quarter-after, then turns the hands to test me, any combination, breakfast time, dinner-time, nap-time, supper-time, going-to-bed-time, midnight-time.

Around and around, day, night, day, night, my father bringing the clock down at six in the morning, putting it up on the warming oven of the stove when he lights the fire, going out to the pasture to bring in the cows, coming in for breakfast, dinner, supper, taking it back up upstairs, ten o'clock, winding it up with the shiny key at the back when he goes to bed, yawning, placing it on his bedside chair where it ticks through quiet darkness of night until it rings again at dawn. I know this routine. Around and around, night day, night day, night day...

"Does time ever stop?" I ask, suddenly seeing in my head everything in front of me vanishing away—my mother bending over me in her soiled white apron, the black stove with its shiny knees, the flustering noon light from the pantry window, the old grey-shingled house we are in, everything, all of outdoors, all of Annapolis County, Kings County, all of overseas vanishing away...

"Only when the world ends," my mother says.

"When?" I ask, afraid.

"Doomsday," she says.

"What's doomsday?"

"Judgment day."

Judgment day when the black whirling hands of the clock in my mother's hands stop, when everything vanishes, disappears, when everything sinks through the floor and becomes a blank ...

"But not for a long time yet," my mother says, her blue eyes shining down at me, telling me that she sees I am afraid, telling me that she herself is not sure by the way her mouth in the corners is tight with something she does not want to say.

"A lot of things have to happen before then. There have to be a lot of religious wars," she says, putting the clock back on the warming-oven so that she can test the turnips again by piercing them with a long fork.

"What's a religious war?" I ask, picturing in my mind two church steeples like huge white pointed sticks fighting, fighting the way Harold and I fight down on the lawn, when we pretend the long knobbly sticks fallen from the trees are swords.

At first she does not answer. Then, looking away to sudden bright light coming in from the pantry window, she says with a queer little laugh, "There've been a lot of religious wars already."

"Christ is supposed to come again," she adds a few moments later.

As if sort of embarrassed.

Janet Parker Vaughan

Fifth Shift

—age three to four—

We are in the front hall standing in bright sunlight. The front door is wide open, the outer storm-door off. As yet no summer screen.

My mother is helping me into most gentle-feeling sleeves, and turning me around to pull the sides of my new orangeypink coat together. With hard fingers she fastens the top button at the hollow of my neck. I am aware that beyond the rosypurple chenille of her long housecoat, beyond the grey wood of the front door sill, birds are twittering for me to get out on the lawn quick. Viola is coming, coming soon from down the road to take me by the hand to early-Sunday-school-church.

But first, floppings of rumpled cuffs about my ears, a settling of the coat's matching orangeypink bonnet around my hair, the straightening of its peak, the tying firm of its wool ties under my chin, all while I look up into my mother's face that tells me by her approving cheeks that she is pleased, more than pleased.

"Now you are ready, Maree-kins," she says, dotingly.

I tip my head down to see the tiny blue and yellow flowers embroidered on my coat's orangeypink breast. I stretch my fingers that barely peek out beyond the ends of the gentle sleeves, caress the coat's soft wool material down to my knees. Oh, the coat cares for me. Its satin lining cares for me tenderly.

"I want people to see how nice you look," my mother says.

Aunt Helen sent the coat, size 3X, and its bonnet in a box of hand-me-downs from the States. Pinned to the coat is a note: 'Barely worn and of good quality'.

"Naturally, Helen would have to say it's of good quality."

Coat and bonnet are "from one of the Turnbull girls, not from Filene's." Turnbulls, she tells me, are high mucky-mucks in Boston.

Deeper inside the box is a whole bunch of rayon stockings that my Aunt Helen cannot wear because they have small holes in the feet. These are for my mother to wear around the house.

"What are filenes?" I ask, putting my hand down into the stirry mess of stockings to look for them, imagining that they are something like the black skipper bugs I have seen scooting around on the surface of the brook-pool by the culvert. But my mother pushes the box and its cover away from my hand.

"Oh, just a name," she says, annoyed. "A bargain-basement store."

*

"I want to show Viola. I want to wait down by the road," I say, slipping past my mother to get myself in my new orangeypink coat and bonnet out onto the grey-splintered wood of the steps, down its three crooked boards, down through the sticky yellow light of the dandelion-sprinkled lawn, down to the road as fast as I can. There to stand under the metal tongue of the mailbox. To wait and watch. Wait for the figure of Viola in her short navyblue coat to come over the western hill.

High above me in the roadside trees, the twittering birds. Enclosing me, branches of dark green-notched leaves that have a bitter smell. Under the stiffness of my bonnet's ties, I feel a bare place on my throat. On the far side of the road, the greygreen trees of the lower orchard fall away in sprawling rows.

I wait, wait. But no Viola comes. I wait so long I do not want her to come. Because I want to walk to early-Sunday-school-church by myself.

I hop from the edge of the lawn to the road's gravel, skip away from the mailbox, quickly cross the mouth of the driveway and its knobbles of stones, take the nearest tire-worn lane alongside the moonberry hedge that will put me out of sight of the house.

I'm on my own, I think to myself.

I will not look back.

I do not want Viola showing up behind me over the hill.

Out on the road, the sun feels warmer still, and its light is so bright that when I look out through holes in the southside trees and then look down, I see all over the road small floating shadows of bedazzled crowns.

"On my own, on my own," is my song.

On my own skipping and hopping and singing past the culvert-brook, under the branches of the northside oaks, past the secret grey boards of the east orchard bridge, more and more feeling the pull and sting of my garters under the layers of my coat, dress, slip, garters with metal fasteners that are suspended from my waist in long tight elastic strips, that dig ugly into the tops of my legs, that more, more, make me push against them, push my white stockinged-legs further than they have ever been.

I am away past the east orchard bridge before I stop to catch my breath, loosen the itchy ties of my bonnet, slide it off my head, shake out my ticklish hair, start on my way again swinging the bonnet by its ties to get on past the borderline fence. Walk, stop, catch my breath, start again all the way to the top of the eastern hill, along, over and down the other side into the deep cold shade of the hollow and over its dark mud bridge, on up the bright gravel slope, along, over and down and up, over bright gravel and shaded gravel almost the whole mile to early-Sunday-school-church. Just before the church, a shiny black car comes up behind me. It's Mr. Wheelock, the Sunday-school-church superintendent, and his wife from down the road. He leans out the window to ask me to hop in. I shake my head "No."

"I'm on my own, I'm on my own," I say.

*

I know my mother loves me. When her feet are cold in bed, and I am not too sick, I try to make them warm by snuggling way down under the covers to put my warm feet on her clammy ones. Then she calls me her little toaster. Her good little girl. Her little honeybunch. Her little Maree-kins.

I am good, but sometimes I am wilfully, purposely horrid: I scream and yell to get something I want. Not because I really want whatever it is, but because I want to feel what it is like to be horrid. My mother seems to know this. "No need to throw a tantrum," she says calmly. Then, she teases me by saying the rhyme she knows I want her to say:

> *There was a little girl who had a little curl*
> *Right in the middle of her forehead;*
> *When she was good she was very very good*
> *But when she was bad she was horrid.*

I only really fight with Harold.

I expect my mother to wait on me, to do things for me, to feed me and read to me, to wash my hands and feet and press my clothes, to sleep with me when I am sick, to change my bed. She likes doing these things for me. She does not like doing these things for the men.

"I don't mind doing things for you kids," is what she says.

Like everyone else in the house, one night a week, instead of the daily sponge bath in the warm kitchen's sink, I have a bath in the cold bathroom upstairs in the big white slippery tub that has claws for feet. Here in an inch of warm water, I slide and slurch up and down, turn over and swim awkwardly on my stomach on the enamel, sit up and make the water murky by rubbing between my hands a hard-edged chalky cake of soap. Then, I reach up to the wire soap dish for my squishy orange rubber duck, spend time squeezing it to suck water up through the metal hole in its bottom, squeezing it out again to shoot droozling water down my stomach. And when the water cools, getting over on my knees to pull the black rubber plug, to watch it spin bluish out of sight down the drain.

Then, shivering, I yell as loud as I can so my mother down in the kitchen will hear me, "Come and dry me!"

After a long interval (I yell loudly several times), I hear her slowly climb the stairs until she finally arrives through the door in a wave of cold air, a weighted presence that wears a soiled apron smelling of dishwater.

Reaching for the thin white towel on the rod on the far side of the sink, she drapes it over her shoulder, then bends over me in the tub to steady me, help me and my slippery nakedness out over the high enamelled side, telling me to be careful not to kill myself, because the tub on its animal feet is high and dangerous and I might crack my skull.

Before my feet have time to enjoy the loops of the mat beside the tub, she throws over me the thick yellow towel from the side of the vanity table, steers me dripping and shivering through the cold of the hall to the bedroom, my feet leaving damp marks on the linoleum. There on the bed, tingly, naked, the yellow towel a faint warmth under me protecting the bedspread, I flail my arms and jounce the mattress, jounce my legs toward her face to make it as hard as I can for her to dry my legs and capture me.

"Oh, you can't get away from me," she laughs, pulling the thinner towel from around her neck to grab one of my kicking legs and rub it dry for dear life. I struggle and twist, think nothing of kicking as hard as I can with my other leg at her soiled-aproned breasts. But that kicking leg she grabs, too, and uses it like a pole to turn me over on my side.

"Oh, no, you don't!" she says.

So does my mother like to struggle and turn and twist. Her breath in the cold room is eager, her hard cool hands are strong, her blue eyes glow. I struggle, struggle to escape. But, letting one leg go and holding one leg high, she reaches down and with the damp end of the towel pats dry the soft dent of my vagina.

"Such a nice innocent-looking little place," she says.

*

It is three o'clock on a winter afternoon. The quilt my mother lies under is pale mauve and covered in ties of fuzzy white yarn. The best quilt in the house which at noon she lifted out of the window-seat in the cold upstairs hall, saying as she shuffled its bulk around the hall chimney, "I am too sick to go on."

Here in my room, she threw it over the bed, making it as even as she could, before turning away to the second drawer of the bureau to find her best nightgown, me watching her draw the old faded flannel nightgown she had on back over her head, to stand naked, ready, to pull the best one down over her large staring breasts, her plump stomach, her faint-brown triangle of hair, letting its flimsy material fall away full and free around her blue-veined legs—her best blue silk nightgown with 'the lace inset'.

"Why?"

Nightgowns are only changed on Saturday night.

"In case the doctor has to come," she says.

*

My brother and I stand at the foot of the bed staring at her, our mother. Harold with his head over the brown metal railing. Me, staring through the brown tube bars. I cannot see her face. Her browngrey hair on the pillow looks mussy.

The light upon the mauve tunnel of her body, like the winter light in the window behind us, seems wan.

Our mother is going to die.

"Call 17-02," she whispers over the hem of the sheet to my brother.

Call Mr. Foster at the corner of the Saunders Road and ask him to go down to the apple warehouse by the railroad track where our father is working for the afternoon, tell him to go down and ask our father to come home.

"Tell him to tell him," she whispers, "That I've never been so sick in my life."

Harold goes downstairs. I stand waiting at the end of the bed until he comes back up. "Stay away," she says, feebly waving her hand as I move to stand closer. Not to catch what she has.

We both stand back. My brother as far away as the window, taking one side of its white-dotted net curtains to twist it into a hank. Me against the crisp white-dotted folds of the dressing table skirt, my head just below the bosom-board of its plywood top where the folds, gathered under a narrow blue ribbon, begin to flow down. We stand and watch. Then, she whispers to us to come closer to the bed.

"If I die," she whispers. "If I die...I want you to promise...Promise me, both of you, that when you grow up you will never drink or smoke."

We stare at our mother lying there, her mussy head on the pillow, her sunken eyelids, her mouth closed in a fading blue line. I think to myself I should be crying, crying because my mother is dying. But I do not feel like crying. I try to cry, but tears will not come. Our mother is dying and she is not saying she loves us. She is not asking Harold to phone 17-02 again, to tell Mr. Foster to go down to the apple warehouse, take a message to our father to tell him she loves him.

"I don't want to drink or smoke," I say, feeling a need to take up for myself.

Sixth Shift

—age four to five—

"You are never to go to the barn alone!" my mother says.

Her voice has force.

"Now, missus," my father says.

But before chores he takes me to the barn to show me what has happened so I will know. Something very bad.

Inside the stable door, lifting me against the sharp buckles of his overalls, he carries me, legs dangling, through the munching manurey warmth, down along the dirty clotted tails of the cows to the shadowy far end of the stable, where the horses with their huge muscular rears stand restless, snorting in their stalls. Queen and Prince. Closer to them than I have ever been, so close that not seeing beyond their tails I sense their huge bellies gorged with dangerous-smelling strength.

"See what can happen to you," my father says.

What I've been brought out to see: a huge red-festering sore the size and shape of a horseshoe on Queen's dark haunch. Where Prince has kicked her.

"Don't come out here alone. And don't go near them in the pasture either. They can get nervous," he says.

I stare at Prince, at his tremendous rear, at the terrible strength of his hind legs, at his large iron-edged hoof down in the straw of the gutter that is shaggily tipped toward me. I am too terrified to say a word. Too terrified to draw up my legs. All I can do is cling to my father's shoulder, bite into his shoulders with my fingers for him to carry me quickly, quickly out of the stable, down along the row of dirty windows, out through the stable door, out into the safety of the late afternoon light. Out to where he puts me down by the grey metal milk pails drying on their stakes.

"A horse can kill you," my mother says.

"They can get nervous," my father says.

The sore I have seen on Queen is the same thing that happened to the face of Avard Stoddart's hired man, my mother says.

No, I will never be going near them, I will be staying away, I will never be begging to be lifted above the wooden flaps of their stalls to touch their long gentle-starred faces; no, I will never be asking when they are being hitched for work to be lifted up to their broad backs. No, I will never be going near them. No, I will never be wanting to be kicked in the face, kicked with a wallop of pain so bad that my eyes and my nose and my mouth will be left a hideous bloodied mash.

*

It is very early in the morning. I am in my parents' bedroom standing barefoot on a small cane-seated chair. I am looking out the window into strange red twittering light, down into the dark shadow of the house covering the west side's apple trees and rocks as far as the dim row of line-fence trees. Behind me, my mother lies in bed under a muddled sheet.

"Do you see your father yet?" she asks. "Is he going down for the cows?"

I push my face into the cutting wire of the metal screen, stretch my eyes to try and see the grey-shingled barn.

"It's awful to see a man cry," she mournfully says.

Out in the barn at the far end of the dusky cow stable, Prince in his stall has sunken down. Sunken down and never going to get up again. My father, crying, has come in to tell us this, has gone out again. I wobble around on the chair to see my mother staring dismally into the shadow of the ceiling-slant.

"I'm sad Daddy's sad," I say, with a sunken feeling inside.

"It's a terrible thing for a man to lose his horse," she says.

I wobble around to look out into the house-shadow again, to the tops of the line-fence trees that have suddenly brightened to golden orange wings.

*

Prince is dead because my father, the haying over and before apple picking starts, goes away for a day to Yarmouth. Just one day. Prince is dead because a man from Bolivars' down-the-road, their hired man, came to do the chores and knew no better than to feed a horse oats with water.

"He suffered, he suffered."

"He let me help him as much I could, but he knew."

"He never sank to his knees 'til his last breath."

"I can't go away for a day."

When breakfast comes, these are things my father says, shaking his head.

"Best horse I ever had."

Later in the morning, Mr. Palmer's son comes with his team and hauls Prince away and buries him in a deep hole. My father buys another horse to harness with Queen. She is younger, chestnut-coloured. Her name is Babe.

*

As soon as my mother gets out of the car, my father tells her. He tells her from where we stand on the top porch step just as she is saying thank you to Mrs. Wilhelmina Rumsey, good enough to take her to Women's Institute, good enough to drive her home, just before Mrs. Wilhelmina Rumsey's black car begins to coast away down the driveway.

"Missus, I've hired some help. Someone's come 'round."

My mother, still nodding goodbye, carefully picks her way toward us over the tiny daisies and ugly flat-leaved plants of the driveway's border-ground. She is dressed in a navyblue suit, white blouse with a frill, shiny black patent shoes on her feet, shiny black patent purse hanging from her arm. Her small pink lipsticked mouth is turned down.

"Missus, I've hired someone," my father says again.

"I told you," she says. "I told you I don't want anyone around!"

"A few more potatoes in the pot, another pair of overalls in the wash, all it is!" he says, a sharp tone to his voice, a sharp bright look in his eyes.

"All it is!" she says, her eyes darting from the house to the barn and back again.

"I need help, Missus! You can't have everything the way you like it!"

"What is it I have that I like!" she says holding in her breath, lurching in her high heels toward us up the steps.

"Why can't Daddy have help?" I pipe up.

All the afternoon he has been saying he is going to have help, he is going to have help, saying this while I have been following him around.

"I don't want it. I'm not able, I'm just not able," my mother says in a whisper, a whisper that sounds as if she is choking on a crumb.

"What's the use of talking to you!" my father shouts, jumping past her.

"Well, I'll get on with my damn work!" he yells, eyes flashing up at both of us, angrily hiking away in his workboots up the edge of the driveway with a slap of his cap to the ground.

"You didn't even wait to ask me," my mother whispers after him.

Why does she not want to wash another pair of overalls, put another potato in the pot? Why does she not want to have a hired man around, when Dad needs help? This hired man who is already waiting in the barn, who rode up the driveway earlier, not sitting on his bicycle seat, but keeping himself upright in a bracing kind of stand, strong legs wrenching the pedals around and around.

"Why can't Daddy have help?" I ask again.

Why does she not want what my father wants?

"Your father and his temper!" she spits out, pushing me ahead of her through the gloom of the porch, a gloom that like the green metal washer in the corner smells like old floor cloths.

"Why?" I say again.

My mother sets her purse on the white oilcloth of the kitchen table, opens it, takes a hankie out, closes it with a snap, just as her mouth is closed for not saying anything more. Taking off her navyblue suit jacket, she hangs it around the back of the north-window chair, then, clacking in her shiny black shoes, she crosses the floor to fetch her apron from the hook behind the stove. Without looking at me, she wraps its dingy cloth around her blouse and skirt, fumbling behind her back to make a bow of its ties.

"Only a pair of overalls!" she sputters, heading around the stove to the dining room to get a bowl of cold potatoes from the fridge.

"You just have to put them in the wash," I say meekly.

"I don't want a hired man here!" she snaps. "Your father knows that!"

"I can help," I say.

I like to help with the wash. I like it when my mother pulls the washer out into the middle of the porch and lifts down the big galvanized rinse tub from its nail to set it evenly on the paint-daubed surface of the backless porch chair. I like— even when she says to stay away— to watch her carry the steaming pails of water into the cool air of the porch, water she has not taken from the hotwater tap but has dipped out of the boiler on the hot stove, to fill the tubs.

I like to watch her throw into the washer tub the handfuls of soap flakes that make the suds that give me a feeling of cleanness in my nose. I like to help by handing up bunches of rumpled sheets, limp pillowcases, soiled underwear that she has gathered from the rooms upstairs and thrown on the ragged linoleum floor of the porch in a heap.

I especially like to drag a chair from the kitchen so I can stand and look down on the swishy-swash of the gyrator in the tub, be there to watch my mother steer the wet sheets into the wringer's rolling grip, to watch the suds gush back as they pass through into the rinse tub. When she switches the rollers the other way, I make sure to get down on the floor, so I can see the rinsed sheets, water spewing behind them, fold down into the waiting laundry basket like flattened tongues. Fun.

"I've never been so angry," she says, her voice shaking as she turns on the cold water tap in the sink to let its wiggly stream wash off pieces of potato skin stuck to her hand.

To be good, I go and sit in the chair by the stove in front of the water tank, watch her click back and forth to the woodbox for sticks to feed the stove, to the fridge, to the pantry, to the sink, to the warming oven to take down the black frying pan, her blue eyes flickering, her mouth more and more certain as she returns to the sink to cube salt pork, peel onion, cut potato; more certain still as she stands at the stove, sliding the ingredients by turns off a cracked plate into the heated pan, calming us both with the sound of sizzling, the comforting smell of pork fat, the scraping and chopping and turning of the browning hash, until I am feeling a little sorry I took up for Dad.

After a while, I ask her may I set the table, something she sometimes lets me do, because now I can see over its edge. I am getting older, I am getting bigger. In the fall I will be going to school.

"Can I, may I, set the table?"

"Not tonight," she says.

*

The very next day the new hired man moves in, lugging his khaki duffle bag of belongings into the kitchen. My mother says nothing to him except, "I'm putting you in the southeast room to the right of the top of the stairs."

While he goes out to speak to my father in the barn, I go upstairs with my mother to move Harold's clothes and bedding back to his old northeast room. First, we have to take the embroidered white bedspread off the bed, me helping to fold it before following after my mother into my room where we put it away in the bottom bureau drawer 'to keep it nice'. Then, going back around the corner to the southeast room, we drag 'Mumma's old blackbrown quilt' from its bed, me holding tightly to one snuffy end as we drag it next door to fling it over what was Maxine's pretty bed to make it Harold's again. Finally, we go to the windowseat down at the end of the hall, where, digging into its musty-smelling depth, my mother yanks up into the day's bright light yellowed sheets, rough brown blankets, a sourgreen wrinkled bedspread.

"They'll air out. That's all I'm going to do for him," she says.

"Missus, can you find him a shirt!" my father says, suddenly appearing behind us on the stairs, his capped head showing through the rails. "What he's got's too hot for haying."

My mother drops the bedding on the floor, goes into their southwest room to dig around in the bureau's lower drawer. She brings out two cotton shirts, a palebrown one that is missing buttons that she is going to have to sew on and an old white one ripped in the sleeve that she is going to have to go to work and mend.

"You wait and see missus, it's going to work out."

"Puh!" my mother says.

"He'll be a great help."

My father winks at me.

My mother says 'puh' again.

*

The new hired man's first name is Sylvestor. "Syl for short," he says, but my mother says she will call him by his full name. His last name he says is Parmenter. Which is sort of like Palmer's name next door put together with the word carpenter. (I have just learned at early-Sunday-school-church that Jesus is a carpenter.)

"Where do you come from, Sylvestor?" my mother asks, handing him his tea cup on that first night. He says he is from down the other way but that he is just back from New Brunswick.

"I was wai-aay across the Bay of Fundy," he says, with a grin, making Harold laugh at him.

I notice that this Sylvestor Parmenter eats by putting a lot of food into one side of his cheek, and that when he smokes after supper he keeps his cigarette to one side of his mouth, blowing out the smoke with an ugly jut to his lower lip. I notice he smells of sweat and hay and cigarettes and that when he bends to the floor to pick up a match near my feet his hair smells like bad breath. I notice he has a crimp in the front of his hair that makes him look like Maxine's Reg.

"His eyes have a smirky look," my mother says.

*

Evenings after chores, after the sun sets behind the mountain, in the glow of light that soon brings in the damp air, Sylvestor plays with Harold and me out on the turn-table lawn at the back of the house. Lots of things he can do, smooth and lean and quick, with a knowing jerk of his head. He can drop swiftly to the grass in his pale haying-shirt and heavy work pants, so that we can roll on top of him and maul him. He can jump up nimbly to chase us, catch us, swing us around and around by our hands, dip us low over the dizzying, darkening ground with a great straining of the veins of his arms. He can play hide-and-seek, tag.

He can roll around with Harold up there by the side of the old horsebarn-garage in the thick sneezy clumps of grass.

"A darn good worker," my father says.

"Just someone I have to have around," my mother says.

"He's just a big kid," she sniffs.

I do not mind Sylvestor. I do not mind that he is a big kid. That when there is a card party and Mum and Dad go away for the evening down to Pleasant Valley Hall, he lets us fool around on his bed. There under the southeast room's ceiling slant, me in my nightgown, Harold in his pyjamas, Sylvestor in sweaty undervest and old grey pants, we wrestle with him the same as we do out on the lawn. I do not mind that he teases us by singing nursery rhymes.

"I know rhymes! I know rhymes!" I gleefully shout.

I know lots of nursery rhymes out of the tattery Mother Goose book my mother keeps in the cubby hole and sometimes still reads to me even though now I can read them for myself.

"Shut up!" Harold says.

"Hickory dickory dock the mouse ran up the clock!" I smartly shout.

The trouble is Sylvestor will not sing the rhymes clearly; he wants to sing them silly, humming them under his breath, like secret words, so we cannot hear them.

"What are the words, sing the words!" Harold and I both shout.

To force him to sing the words out loud, we crawl over him on the bed, tussle with his hard twisting leanness, Harold elbowing me out of the way, me squirming around on Sylvestor's back to pinch him as hard as I can through his vest, a thin slopey undershirt, that shows the line of the tan on the back of his neck, the white pumps of muscles on his upper arms.

"Say them, say them!" Harold insists, pounding at him.

"Say the words slow, say the words slow!" I demand, falling over his neck in a somersault to the nasty roughness of the blankets that my mother says are "good enough for the likes of him."

Sylvestor, big kid, does not mind at all us how much we tom-fool with him, 'try to get his goat', tumble over him in helpless, huffing, never-ending wrestle. He just pulls away from us every once in a while and sits with his legs dropped over the side of the bed. One rhyme he mutters has something to do with an eighteen pounder, something about the white of an egg that comes from an eighteen pounder.

"It's Humpty Dumpty!" I exclaim.

"Don't tell her, don't tell her," Harold says laughing, pummelling the back of Sylvestor's shoulders with his fists.

It does not take me long to get suspicious that the words Sylvestor will not let us hear are bad words, like the words about going to the bathroom are bad words, like the words you are not supposed to say about boys' parts are bad words.

"Never say dink," my mother says. "No matter what the boys or anyone else says. And don't say bottom, say BTM."

BTM is what Mrs. Whynott, the lady who lives next door, says.

"Never say kaa," my mother says one day, when I am flushing the toilet in the bathroom, watching what I have with effort pushed out of myself go whirling cleanly out of sight down the enamel bowl of the drain. I do not want to say kaa anyway.

A word I have heard Aunt Edna say twice. "Do you want to go kaa-kaa?"

A bad word I do not like the sound of. That makes me feel like a baby. That makes me feel ashamed.

"Say stool," my mother says.

Stool sounds no better.

"No matter what you hear other kids say. I don't ever want to hear you say such words," my mother says. If I do, I can tell from her voice, I will be very bad and she will be very upset.

I do not know what other kids say. Because the only kids I know are at early-Sunday-school-church, where you would never, never say bad words. I only know what Harold and our friend Peter, who lives in the old Abner Foster place up the road, say. They say dink on the road when they pee with their little white hoses, and laugh.

I do not pee on the road. If I have to pee, I squat and wet from my secret innocent place in the hiding ditch.

"I don't even want you to say pee. Say wet instead."

There are even worse bad words that the boys snicker about, shit for stool, piss for wet and some word like uck for I do not know what. Also, it is worse to say words out of church for swear words, like God Almighty or Jesus Christ.

But out in the barn I have heard Dad lots of times say "Jesus Christ!"

Another bad word is ass. Peter says it is a bad word meaning bottom, but not if it means donkey, like the ass-donkey Mary rode on in the Bible to go to Bethlehem.

Why are some words good and not good, some words so secret and bad you are never to say them? Why do some words that are good sound bad? Why does vagina, the good name for my girl's place, sound bad? Why are words about going to the bathroom bad? Is it not good to go to the bathroom and get it over with? I do not understand.

"Why can't I know?" I ask, wanting to know about the eighteen pounder.

"Don't tell her! Don't tell her! She's a girl!" Harold yells in Sylvestor's ear, coming in behind him to try and push him head-first off the edge of the bed.

"What's it stand for? What's it mean?" I ask Sylvestor, asking him the same questions my mother asks when she is teaching me how to read, when she points at letters, like 'p' for 'puh' or words like ocean that is another name for sea.

"Come 'ere, I'll whisper it to ya," Sylvestor says with a big grin, wresting himself away from Harold's grip to stand clear of him down on the floor in his grey wool sock-feet.

I scramble down, move with Sylvestor around the bottom of the bed, so he can bend over me and fuh into my ear a word that sounds like muck. The word that Harold and Peter snicker about?

Fuh-uck ?

"What is it? What it is!" I demand, not sure I have heard right the word Harold does not want me to know.

"Don't tell her! Don't tell her!" Harold yells from the bed.

So Harold will not hear, Sylvestor cups his mouth to my ear and whispers.

"I'll show ya sometime," he says.

*

On the night I am shown, I am in bed early and my mother comes into my bedroom to say a special goodnight before she and my father drive away. First she draws the blind, because the sun, low now on the ridge of the mountain, is setting the orangeypink wallpaper of the room ablaze.

"You'll never sleep," she says.

She bends toward me over the low bed to give me her goodnight kiss but, like every night she goes out, she cannot quite reach my cheek, because the girdle she is wearing underneath the silky feel of her slip, under the pale flowery cotton of her summer dress, makes her stiff.

"Goodnight, honeybunch," she says, tucking the sheet in around my shoulders.

"Night, Mummy," I say.

I always call her Mummy just before I go to bed, before she turns to go out of the room, before she leaves me, shuts the door as far as it will go without a thud, before, with satisfied heels, she slowly taps her way down the steps.

She has said nothing about what I already know. Harold will be going over to Peter's for a while and I will be in the house with Sylvestor alone.

I wait, hearing the engine of the truck start up on the other side of the house, listen to its wheels crackle down the gravel, to the jerk of the gears down at the bottom of the driveway, to the sound of the truck's gear-changes as they head up the road.

I lie awake, like I always do, to watch the brightening in the orange blind fade. I listen to the empty hall outside the closed door, because I know sure as sure, as soon as Harold has gone from the kitchen, Sylvestor's foot-steps will be on the stair, that he will be coming up rightaway, will show me the word I want to know, will ask me to come into his room. I do not know how I know.

*

A few mornings later, my mother and I are in Sylvestor's room making the bed. The bottom end of the top sheet is yanked out from where it should be tucked under the end of the mattress.

"This mattress is not that old but it smells mousey just the same," my mother complains.

Then both of us see at the same time a bunch of something, something satin pink lying at the foot of the bed, as though pushed there by Sylvestor's feet. My pink satin underpants from the night that Sylvester said he had something to show me in his room, that from under my nightgown I took off. That I forgot.

I am very afraid. The thing that he did, the bad word I am not supposed to say, the faster and faster motion he did up and down with his big thing, leaving a big sneeze like the white of an egg all sticky over my thighs and between my legs.

"Don't tell anyone what we did, now will ya," he said, wiping at his thing with a red polka-dot handkerchief.

"Why what are your panties doing here!" my mother exclaims. "How come they're in Sylvestor's bed!"

"Must be left from putting away the wash," I say, thinking quick, knowing I am thinking quick. Just something from the wash that slipped down out of sight, slipped down there the late afternoon of washday when my mother plunked down a stack of clothes fresh from the line on Sylvestor's green bedspread, things that only needed to be straightened and folded, did not need to be ironed: towels, nightgowns, pyjamas, underwear, socks for putting away.

On tiptoe, I reach up and slither the underpants out from under the sheet so my mother will not see they are not clean, were not in the wash on washday, slither them out, bunch them up in my hands so my mother can go ahead, reach down and tuck the loosened end of the sheet back in between the mattress and the low end of the bed. So that when she walks up and down her side, I can walk up and down my side, holding the panties out of sight, my other hand reaching to pull up on the hem of the thin mousey sheet, straightening it so that next can come the blankets, brownish, tough, every so often, me looking up, but not so much that she will notice, every so often looking up at her dotted, thinking eyes.

Can she tell when she looks over at me, when she folds back the hem of the sheet to make it neat, that in my stomach I am very afraid. Can she tell by looking at me that I have lied? Can she know what is in my head?

When the bed is made, while my mother is in the bathroom, I go into my bedroom, the northwest room, where we are going to go next, and put the bunch of satin underpants far back in the middle drawer of the bureau, deep under the mollywog that is there, where my mother's and my things are jumbled together with bunches of knotted stockings, the mollywog of stuff Aunt Helen sent us from the States, messes of slippery underwear.

*

I stand on tiptoe to lift the latch. At that moment, the sun comes out, its light shining through the cobwebby panes of the porch window to show that in the grain of the kitchen door's darkorange wood are yellow streaks. It is the in-and-out light of the sun I have been watching all the way home, one moment brightening the heads of the bare-budded roadside trees, the next darkening the grass, the next showing up dazzling yellow within the day's fast-moving flocks of cloud, light that has been drawing me home against a surprising warmth of wind, making me feel, even though I am badly wheezing from walking fast, that spring has come, that winter is over, that I am growing strong.

I click the latch free, push the door open, do my best to smother back my wheezing. My mother is standing at the stove. She is stirring something with a wooden spoon, wearing the blue apron around her unchanged school clothes that Aunt Frances gave her for Christmas. She is home from her school down the road before I am, and the kitchen is already suppery-warm.

"You're late!" she says, without turning to see me.

By the clock on the top of the stove it is half-past four.

"I've made good potato scallop," she says, stooping to open the oven door, so I can see the glass dish, its creamy bubbling, its top layers of potato slices already starting to turn brown.

"You're wheezing," she scolds. "Why do you always have to run!"

"Late...playing... at Peter's."

I want to say, cannot say, do not have enough breath to say that I did not run home, I just walked fast, happy-fast in the wind, all the way home looking up at the brightening and darkening of the clouds, the ins-and-outs of the sun.

"I'm making good chocolate pudding," she says. She puts her stirring spoon on the door of the warming oven, turns to help me out of the straps of my bookbag.

"Why where are your stockings!" she says, noticing that my legs stand cold and bare in my new spring rubber boots.

"In...my...pocket," I say, looking down at the big bulge in the side of my coat.

"You took them off!" she says crossly, putting her hand in the pocket to draw them out. But they are stuck badly together at the knees where I fell in the burdocks.

"I got...sweaty-hot," I say. "I took... them...off."

Sweaty-hot from running around in Peter's yard, playing tag with Harold and Peter in the warm afterschool wind, running around and around Peter's playhouse, around its back wall through old hay and rusted machinery and grasping burdocks, around to the front, running, wheezing, over the flat stones of the woodshed walk, through the thick dooryard grass, running, wheezing, very hot in my long flapping coat that I had to take off, throw to the ground, running in my red plaid skirt and red sweater, my waist, that holds up my stockings, tightening against my breathing, my sweaty-hot chest...very sweaty-hot.

"And what's this! Your waist!" my mother exclaims, seeing the bump in the other pocket. "Why, you've taken it off!"

She yanks it out, cramped undergarment of long white elastic garters, shining metal-keepers and rubber knobs.

"You aren't able to take this off by yourself!"

"The boys...helped me...take it off. They un...hooked me. They wouldn't...help me...put it back on..."

Would not help me, would not stop to help me, when I wanted to start for home. I look up into my mother's eyes with the truth. What I am told at Sunday school church. Always tell the truth.

But my mother's blue eyes do not look down into mine. They are staring over my head through the open kitchen door into the spring-light of the porch. And I know what they are thinking, they are thinking that the boys wanted to look at me, show me something, like that Sylvestor-man, who was here in the summertime to hay, wanted to show me something without my panties on.

"The boys should not be taking your clothes off! I don't like this at all."

"I was...sweaty hot," I say again, starting to cry.

She is not believing me. And I know what she is going to do.

"Don't...tell Dad...Don't...tell...Dad!" I beg, I plead.

 "Don't tell him...don't tell him!" I cry.

He will be mad, very mad. I know he will be mad.

"I want...to go to bed...I'm sick...I feel sick," I sob.

I run out of the kitchen through the hall door. I run down the hall to go upstairs, to pretend I am sick, to hide.

*

I get out of my wool skirt and sweater into my nightie. I get into bed, pull the cool top sheet over my face. I will pretend it is not suppertime with good potato scallop and chocolate pudding. I will pretend it is dark night.

But down in the kitchen, I hear my father's voice. He is in from the barn. He is in the porch. He is talking to my mother. I hear her voice mumbling. She is telling him, I know she is telling him the boys took my clothes off.

I hear him coming, his workboots clomping through the downstairs hall, clomping up the stairs. I turn my face to the wall. I am asleep, a sleep so deep I can never be woken.

"What's this I hear, you and the boys!" he roars, arm smashing the door wide.

"Turn and face me!" he yells, his rough fingers pinching my cheek to turn me, make me look up at the blaze in his eyes.

"The boys...took my...waist off," I cry, knowing I am blaming them for what they did not really do.

"Don't ever let me hear you doing the likes of that again," he yells.

"Do you hear me?" he yells louder. "Never again!"

As abruptly as he has come in the room, he leaves.

"By the Lord Harry," he shouts, thumping back down the stairs.

I cry, cry with terrible high-pitched whining, terrible retchings, shudderings, sobs, cry with tears that drench my pillow, burn my cheeks, swell my eyes into burning slits. My father thinks I am very bad. My father thinks I have shown myself to the boys, like I showed myself to that Sylvestor-man who was here. I cry until I can no longer cry. I stare, stare forever toward the orangey light, the brightening light, the fading light of the slow-dying blind.

Janet Parker Vaughan

Seventh Shift

Part I

—age three to five—

I waddle over sparkling white crust. Above my head, dark blue sky. Through the spindles of trees down by the road, the dazzling light of the sun. I cannot see much. I pass under the pantry window, stay close to the east wall's shabby grey shingles, make my way to the house corner. I do not want my mother to see me.

I know where I want to be—by the cellar doors, inside the frozen snowdrift that is shaped like a saucer. I crawl up and over its icy rim, slide face-down into its shining white protection.

Long time I sit there, legs and boots straight out to the front of me, eyes squinting, my knitted hat heating my head, my bottom under me growing cold. Around my mouth a tied-tight wool scarf, hurting my nose. I tug at it, yank it down with mittened hands, then shift forward onto my knees to look over the saucer's rim to see the bluish tracks of the driveway, the white-brocaded slope that falls away from its edge to the frozen brook below, the hill on the other side of the brook that rises glitteringly into orchard rows of bare-limbed trees that stand in bluish coves.

Long time I kneel, snow-sweet air tingling the inside of my nose. Listening. For crows.

"Those old February crows."

Which my mother and I see from the pantry window, that sail down on black flaps of wings from the mountain woods, cawing noisily, touching down to strut on hardened white drifts almost out of sight up by the dump.

"Caw, caw," I would like to hear.

But no sounds today, no "caw, caw."

Only a shriek. That makes me stretch up from my knees, turn in my bulky suit to look down the lawn.

Old Mister Blue Jay, who I know, who I see every day from a chair in the front room window, who lives in the scabby grey branches of the maple tree, flies from it like a burning-blue arrow over the snow. I squint, look hard to see him, but the light of the morning is too strong.

I listen again, eyes squeezed closed. A tiny voice I wait for, tiny seedy voice from across the brook, from far away in trees by the road, tiny voice that speaks to me, only me, so far away, so near, "Chickadee dee dee, chickadee dee dee."

*

We are walking, my brother and I, over the eastern hill. Each of us on our own darkened strip of tire track, each of us on our own strip of polished hardness. Either side of us in the road's pink gravel are small glinting stones. The sun directly above is hot on our heads. Our bare feet are uncomplaining, soundless.

Steadily we are walking, no fooling around. We want to get there. We want to see him. The boy who has moved in. The somebody we are going to play with.

Me, I can stretch my legs to match my brother's legs, stride for stride. I can do this. Yes, I can. Steadily we are walking, down the hill into the hollow, down into cooling shadows, down to the wooden rails of a bridge, where, when I look up into the leaves of trees far above, I see a great green glow. Leaves, on this windless day, which are silent.

We know what his name is. Peter Saunders. And his mother is Alice, born up North Shore way, and his father is Norman, who is back from the war. And they are going to live in the old Abner Foster place, the big white double house, just before the schoolhouse, that has two front doors.

"Now, don't stay too long," my mother said. "Just say hello. They're just moving in."

Steadily we walk out of the hollow, up the slope of brown-packed mud that under foot is cool and calm.

*

Harold knocks on the wood of the side-door screen. I do, too.

"Don't," Harold says.

We stand, sunheat on our shoulders, a smooth slab of stone under our feet.

A patch of white blouse appears, then an arm opening the screen on a whine, making us stand back as far as we can, then a pair of white perforated tie-shoes and a blue skirt, then a lady with a smile who has blonde hair shaped like Harold's winter helmet.

"You must be Harold and Marion, come in!" she says.

We are pleased she knows who we are, just as we know who she is.

We step over the worn sill into a small hall of blotched wallpaper that smells like scorch, follow her through into a darkness where we cannot see much of anything.

"Find yourselves places to sit, if you can," this Mrs. Saunders says, going out of sight somewhere.

I get up on a shadowy hump near the door. It is a trunk like the one that sits in the hired man's room at home, that has rounded hurtful ridges. Harold keeps on going, steers through boxes and crates toward the green glow of a window at the end of a white metal table that stands in behind me. The boy is in here somewhere.

I see him. Down where the brown-ribbed wall that is becoming visible opposite me turns a corner. He is kneeling behind a cardboard box, and lifts his head to show a yellow tuft of hair, then a blue eye, as his mother asks him to see who is here.

"Peter, say hello! This is Harold and Marion."

"Hello," he says, drawing back out of sight.

"They've come to visit from down the road," his mother says.

"Hello," Harold and I say, polite.

He comes out behind the box and moves toward Harold to reach for something at the end of the table, a small blue-striped tube. He holds it up to his face and aims it like a pea-shooter straight at me.

"What is it?" I ask, frightened.

"A collide-o-scope," he says, turning to point it at the window.

A sort of telescope, a small one, like Harold and I make out of the tubes of calendar holders? I scramble down off the trunk, hurting my leg on a buckle.

"Shake it," this Peter boy says, handing it to Harold.

Harold shakes it. "It sounds like gravel."

Harold puts it to his eye, turns it round and round in his hands as if trying to see something outside in the window's green leaves.

"Bits of glass," this Peter says, taking it back to look through it again.

Bits of glass in the tube or in the leaves?

"So," Harold says, not liking it.

"I want to see!"

"Don't give it to her," Harold says.

"I'm almost four!" I say.

Peter hands it to me.

I hold it to my eye, but I don't see anything.

"Squint your other eye," he says.

But I can't squint the other eye.

"Hold it up."

"I am holding it up."

"Hold it up, dunce!" Harold says.

Again I hold the tube to my eye, tilt it toward the window. Covering my open eye with my free hand, I turn the tube the best I can, until I am seeing what they have been seeing, a star, a glowing beauty-star, glowing tiny mirrors of colours, purple, orange, white, green, a beauty-star that gives me a queer feeling in my chest. Like an ache.

"Turn the tube!"

"Turn the tube!"

I turn it, see the colours collide, change shape, make another star, more darkly glowing, orange star of evergreens and purple night.

"Stars!" I say wonderingly.

"Mirrors, bits of coloured glass," Peter explains.

"Let me see it again," Harold says, taking it from my hand.

*

And then we are walking home, Peter coming with us over the hill to see where Harold and I live, three pairs of bare feet that climb out of the clammy hollow, three pairs of bare feet that bear down flatly over the top of the hill onto leaf-dappled gravel, Harold taking the northside and its shiny spotted track under the tall spruce bank, Peter and I on the southside, walking along in stretches of sunshine, me a little behind, my inside foot on the track's hard smoothness, my outside foot on roughness of gravel.

"We're not the same age," Harold says.

 I'm six," Peter says.

"I'm almost four!" I say.

"Doesn't matter how old you are," Harold says. "You're not old enough!"

"I am so!"

"Well I'm going on eight," Harold says, breathing out a sigh.

Three pairs of bare feet walking over the leaf-dappled hill, past Palmers', past their lawn of fading purple lilacs, down the long sun-struck slope, underneath the high bank of their gnarled orchard, past the rows of our east orchard hidden behind the roadside oaks, three pairs of bare feet leveling out over the culvert of the quiet brook, on by the dark green moonberry hedge, three pairs of feet walking to the bottom of our driveway to where Harold and I live.

Where we look up. At a shabby old house with a grey east wall of messy green vines. At a house that has a mouth of crooked grey steps, a front-door nose of streaked boards, and four sleepy eyes of paned-windows that look down at us from under half-drawn green blinds: shabby old house. Not a white-shingled house, pretty-faced and trim, like Whynotts' house next door or Palmers' house or Fosters' house where this Peter lives...ours a shabby old grey-shingled house that sits atop a sneezy white field of dandelions.

"Our house is old," I say to Peter.

Old and grey. Like old Mrs Fenerty and her house down the road.

"It's grey," Peter says, frowning up at it.

"My mother's going to fix it up," I say.

"So what?" Harold says.

"Never mind, I like dandelion puffs," Peter says, picking one from the edge of the lawn and blowing on it.

The three of us watch the airy bits of fluff drift out of sight in the tall grass along the edge of the driveway.

*

All summer, this first summer with our new Peter friend, we visit back and forth between our houses, our three pairs of tanned bare feet treading fast along the road's surface of stinging hot gravel, sometimes in mid-afternoon coming home the back way, (according to Harold and Peter, the 'old west' way), traipsing over rough pasture land along the foot of the mountain, following along sometimes one side, sometimes the other, of sagging lines of fences, stumbling, panting through thick grass along the tops of sprawling orchard rows, finding, on days we climb higher, pale strips of cow path that speed us over great humps of mountainside down through rocks and sprawling juniper to our fence, our brook and home.

Some mornings we play in either of our brooks, splashing after slippery green frogs, some afternoons red light or giant steps or red-rover-come-over on either of our front lawns. Sometimes we play cowboys and Indians. I am the Indian.

"No need of playing inside the house," our mothers say.

Unless it is pouring rain.

Hot summer afternoons we are often at Peter's, following up the ruts of the old orchard behind his house, stealthily moving up through its gloomy tunnels of trunks toward the bright spots of light far above, up through its sprawling, uneasy dampness as if on earth no other time, no other place than its deep rotting shade, the dank contentment of its sullen grasses.

*

Every afternoon by four I am home lying on a nubbed flannel sheet on the front room sofa, crying with terrible pains in my stomach and legs. Terrible pains that make me moan and groan, helplessly cry until, thumb in my mouth I stare, float away to sleep. Every afternoon my mother comes in from the kitchen to sit beside me, saying, always saying, what I do not want to hear,

"You are tired out from following the boys."

"No, I'm not, no I'm not."

"I'm strong, I'm strong," I always moan back.

Every afternoon at four I cry and moan and groan and fall asleep, until at five I wake up to dance around the dining room table to the tune of the Ocean Wave, the fishermen's broadcast.

*

My boots are on, my coat is on, I want the ties to my hat done now. I have a secret idea. I want to go and play down on the lawn in the bright colours of leaves that are falling from the trees. I want to go in my new brown coat and new green hat and gather them. I want to give them to my mother.

"I guess old Jack Frost was out last night," my mother says, giving the ties to the hat a tighter yank. Said with her funny little laugh, that today is like a little motor that starts up with a wobble, then stops.

I stare up at the shine in her blue eyes that says she is as pleased with my new hat as I am. My hands reach up to feel it on my head, this my hat that Aunt Edna knit me, that fits me, caps my head gently—except for the tightness of the strings under my chin. Its colour is like the boughsweet apple I ate at Grammie Grave's place, that was softgreen and pithy in my mouth, that I liked.

97

"Edna when she's on night shift at the hospital has lots of time to knit," my mother says.

Aunt Edna is a nurse; she is able to do things, my mother says, because she has no little kids.

"I'm going now," I sing out, turning away from her eyes, away from her dingy rayoned legs, her one leg swollen up big.

I have a secret and I step away over the worn sill of the kitchen into the ugly-smelling porch, cross its patched linoleum to the outside door, push up on its jiggy black latch, hauling it open to step outside into the huge light of outdoors that makes me want to run, run around the house corner in the strong wind, run away as fast as I can out of sight of the pantry, my boots thumping past the cellar doors, past the scabby trunk of the maple tree down to the bottom of the lawn, running running as fast as I can, like the gingerbread man, catch me, catch me if you can...little old woman, little old man...

*

Above in the crackling branches is windy cold. Down among the roots where I am is a lull, safe and warm. I sit with my legs straight out, a damp bouquet of bright leaves in my hands, under my bottom the damp of the ground. On the bare part of my leg, between my metal garter and the top of my stocking, the lining of my coat feels soft like the green satin spread on Aunt Frances' bed. Oh, I like this my new coat, that I chin down to see, its bulky front of oatmeal-coloured tweed, its big smooth brown buttons that make me strong.

"Helen says it'll last you a good two years."

"One, two, three…"

I count my leaves, a pat for each colour, each veiny shape, this one small as a finger green and red, this one big as a hand, orangeyred, this one long, notched, golden brown, this one…I pat them, praise them, these beauty leaves that under my fingers feel like maps. I take them up one by one, twiddle them on their stems, rest them one by one against my cheek, place them side by side, glistening with dampness on my lap. Jack Frost painted them. Jack Frost with his invisible brush. Jack Frost who stands on a ladder in a very large place in my head, a place higher than the crackle of the trees, wider than the gusts of the wind.

*

"Mummy, look," I say, holding up my beauty-bouquet.

"O good, your cheeks are nice and red," she says, turning away from the blackness of the stove where, in a cloud of steam, she is sizzling brown-smelling meat.

"I'll press them after dinner," she says.

"I don't want you to press them!"

"Put them on the pantry window," she says.

"It's a bouquet for you, Mummy," I say.

Secret beauty-bouquet.

"Don't you like it, Mummy?"

I push its colours up toward her face.

"Here, take your boots off," she says.

"For you, Mummy," I say.

"Pretty," she says.

After dinner she presses them, setting up the ironing board in the middle of the floor, placing them between waxpaper sheets, stomping down on them one by one with the hot black iron that sits on the back of the stove.

"I don't want you to! I don't want you to!" I cry.

"You'll keep them this way."

"I don't want to keep them!"

She lets me see one, puts one in my hand, warm and smeared, smelling of wax, its red colour ruined with a queer sort of shining.

"You can keep it in the dictionary," she says.

I do not want to keep it in the dictionary. I want it damp and glistening and beauty-red, the way I found it out on the lawn. I want it like in the bouquet, the way I brought it in. I can't stop crying.

"You'll be doing this sort of thing at school, making things," my mother says, clomping the iron down again.

"I don't want this sort-of-thing at school!" I rage.

But I do want to go to school, where the boys are all day, where Maxine is. I want to be in the school, the peaked white building on the other side of Peter's east orchard, where there are other kids.

"You're just lonely for the boys," my mother says.

"No I'm not!"

"I always get a lonely-feeling in the fall, too," my mother says.

*

"Looks like Jack Frost really came last night," my mother says.

She holds me up under the armpits to see through the panes of the pantry window how the faded grass of the hollow is coated with white fur and humpled-over stiff.

"You can't go outside today," she says. "The air will chill your lungs. You'll have to stay in. "

"You are good about keeping yourself occupied, so I can get on with my work," she says, moving away..

My mother's work is scraping pots in the sink, washing, starching, ironing, folding, hanging clothes up on lines out to the west side of the house. Her work is scrubbing with the swishy grey string mop, sweeping, making beds, mixing floury bread in the pantry, putting a flat red roast in the oven in a blackened metal pan, peeling carrots and potatoes, going back and forth to the woodbox for wood, clanging the lid of the stove, rolling out pastry for spy-apple pies.

"You don't always have to go outdoors. There's lots of things for you to do inside."

Nothing to do but sit on the floor and play tinker-toys.

"No, there isn't!" I cry.

*

Nothing to do in the afternoon, when the kitchen after two o'clock has an empty brown light, when my mother goes into the cold of the living room to water plants, comes out again and shuts the door, sits at the kitchen table after three o'clock with a pen and a slim mottled-grey book that has a whole lot of envelopes sticking out of it. Nothing to do except on the days she makes a fire in the living room stove and ladies with high-pitched voices come in stamping their boots in the swept-out porch. Ladies who come to work on the purple and yellow quilt that is set up at the far end of the living room on poles, a frame. Mrs. Winnie Palmer, Mrs. Cora Henderson, Mrs. Ida Foster. Who laugh.

Nothing to do when snow is blustering about the house, filling in the panes of the windows so we cannot see out, nothing to do while we wait for Harold to return from school, for Dad to come stomping into the porch from packing apples in the warehouse, for Maxine to show up brown-haired and snowy-scarfed, taller than the kitchen door, nothing to do but for my mother and me to sit side-by-side in chairs pulled up to the kitchen stove, our legs and beaded-slippered feet stretched into the dark heat of the open oven door.

Sometimes she wants me to sit on her lap. I do not want to sit on her lap. I do not like the feel of sliding off.

"But you're Mummy's little honeybunch," she says, with her little laugh.

I do not want to be her little honeybunch, like I am something sweet, like golden plums of syrupy preserves, to be slurped up. I want my mother in her chair, me in my chair, so I can look up and see her long pale cheek, see her blue eyes glance down to the apron that looks like a round damp field of flowers covering her stomach. I want to see her legs beside mine reaching inside the oven as far as the red bricks which she will wrap in newspaper and carry upstairs after supper to take the chill out of our beds.

"My legs aren't long enough," I complain, so my mother will get up, shuffle around the woodbox side of the stove to the cubbyhole, find last year's catalogue to put on the oven door for me to put my feet on.

*

"I'm going to get something else," she says one day, putting the catalogue down for me, keeping on going beyond the water tank side of the stove to open the dining room door. "May as well," she says.

There is something in the cold dining room she has been saving in a drawer. An old school primer.

"From when I was teaching before you kids were born," she says, coming back to her chair, sticking her feet back in the oven beside mine.

"We'll sound out some words," she says.

She opens the orangeybrown primer and gets me to sound out the words by pointing to the letters. The sounds of the letters I already know. I have been learning them at the Chatauqua board that sits on the windowseat upstairs.

"This one, that one," she says, pointing, until I can read a whole sentence. And then another sentence.

> *Here I am. My name is Nan. I have a doll. I have a pet, too.*
> *My cat's name is Blackie. Blackie likes to play in the leaves.*

Easy!

My mother is pleased. I am pleased.

*

"Tell me a story," I demand, tired of the primer.

I want the story about Red Riding Hood and the Big Bad Wolf who pretends to be grandmother and how the woodcutter comes in the nick of time and cuts off his head. Or the story about The Three Little Pigs and another Big Bad Wolf, who huffs and puffs but cannot blow down the house of the third little pig whose house is made of bricks. Or about Hansel and Gretel who escape from being eaten by the Wicked Witch. Stories. The Little Red Hen and The Gingerbread Man and Goldilocks and The Three Bears, stories that I beg my mother to tell over and over again until her voice falls weak and the fire dies down and our slippered-feet cool off and a chill comes down around our backs.

*

Winter afternoons like this in the kitchen. But many winter afternoons spent in the upstairs hall, where I play on days my father, knowing the night is going to be very cold, lays a fire in the new wood furnace in the cellar, so that warm friendly air wafts up through the stairwell from the black holes of the metal register that has been newly set below in the front hall floor. Also, on afternoons when there is no warmth from the cellar furnace at all. Only a brightening light from the window far above the windowseat that warms my stockinged knees when I sit on the cold linoleum floor. Here I play jail with my new Christmas doll, Mary, using the rails of the stairwell for bars, but mostly I play school.

I play school by standing on a Filene's bargain-basement box stuffed with old clothes to make me tall enough to lean forward over a darkgreen blackboard that lies on the windowseat. A blackboard that has metal rods slanting up to hold upright at its back a shallow case of yellowish wood. Across the lower section of the case is a compartment, made of slats, to hold an erasing cloth, either side of which are circles of wires to hold pieces of chalk. In its upper section is hung a mysterious scroll that looks like two ends of a roll of wallpaper held just so far apart.

To play school, I roll the scroll up and down, stretching up over the blackboard, to take hold of the small black turning knobs on either side. I can roll it all the way to the bottom, I can roll it all the way to the top to show screen after screen of things my mother says are things I can be taught. This the Chautauqua Board my mother says that taught her and her sisters when they were little girls.

My fingers, aching, work hard to turn the stiff knobs, to find the parts of the scroll I like to look at, my mother, coming upstairs to check on me every so often, to ask, "Where are you now?"

Some screens are white, some navyblue, some darkgreen, some have black and white numbers and alphabet letters, some have pictures and flags and 'diagrams'— all to teach me something, my mother says: how to draw, how to print, how to write the Palmer method with your hand and arm going around and around. I do not want to learn about the Palmer method, I want to learn the numbers and letters and what the pictures are, and the 'diagrams'.

The first screen, darkgreen, shows rows of skinny white-lined drawings of a ladder, a house, a teepee, a cat, a watering can, a sundial, a girl with a bonnet, three bears.... these I try to draw for myself on the flat of the darkgreen blackboard with a stubby piece of chalk, doing my best to copy the circles and lines they are made of. I can do the ladder, the cat. I cannot do the girl with the bonnet.

Another darkgreen screen further down shows white, cold-looking silhouette shapes of dogs, cats, turkeys, pigs. These I do not like. I strain to turn the knobs to bring more screens into view, one that shows wavy, colourless pictures of many-petalled flowers that are, my mother tells me, zinnias, dahlias, chrysanthemums. Another that shows an interesting screen of faces, drawings of three bearded men in a row, with them a stern-looking woman who sits beside a child at a table, a woman with a name that sounds sort of like Margarita's.

"That's Montessori," my mother says.

Further down still—tiresome, tiresome the turning to get there—the screen I spend the most time with, one that has numbers on it and two sets of letters of the alphabet that I learn to write on the blackboard, small and capital letters with marks underneath them called dots and dashes.

"That's Morse code."

Down, further down, a screen that frightens me of a black train rushing toward me (like in the movies, my mother says), followed by a screen with pictures of bicycles and old-fashioned cars and distant ocean ships, and of sliding-to-earth aeroplanes with double wings...

"Forms of transportation."

"Papa wanted us girls to be educated," my mother says.

*

Hours I spend standing on the Filene's box, learning the screens, leaning over the blackboard, working my fingers until they are numb, working the hard little knobs to get to the pictures down near the end: to soft rosy-coloured screens of fruits and flowers; gingery-coloured caterpillars, cocoons, moths; brighter-coloured pictures of stiff-looking birds of different sizes and the colours of their eggs, down to the best one of all: the screen that shows the flags of all the countries of the world.

Row upon row of bold bright patterns of red, white and blue; of black, yellow and green; of stars, of stripes: of crosses; of crowns; suns, too, the huge red one of 'warlike Japan'; the flag of Czecho-slovakia, the country where the white-haired Czech people down on the farm with Otto and Margarita used to live; and this one, the red cross of Switzerland, where Margarita's daughters, who maybe do not know where she is, might be; and this one of Spain, where Margarita was born; of Italy, France, the countries whose languages she speaks; this one, our country Canada, "only an ensign" my mother says, red with a yellow crown on it and green leaves and a complicated-looking badge that is hard to see; also the 48 Stars and 13 Stripes of the United States, where Aunt Helen lives and the older brothers and sisters of my father, where my father once lived; the largest flag that waves over top of them all, a red, white, and blue one of crosses crossing, the Union Jack, the flag of Great Britain, which is the flag of Winston Churchill and the King and Queen.

"Where's Hitler's flag?" I ask.

There is no flag for Hitler, for Otto, for Germany.

"Maybe it didn't exist as a country when the Chatauqua Board was made," my mother suggests.

Germany, like me, lived somewhere before in the air?

*

One afternoon, my mother comes up from downstairs to say it is lovely and warm in the kitchen and why am I staying up here in the cold when there is no furnace fire on. I say I am making words. Like she has shown me. All I have to do is put a letter of the alphabet in front of *at* or *ell* or *ing* or *ug* or *ong* to see that I get a *bat* or a *bell* or a *bing* or a *bug* or a *bong*.

Today I have made up a story of Mr. and Mrs. Ell and Mr. and Mrs. Ong who plant gardens, milk cows, live in houses with bugs and dogs, go to church where bells ring ding-dong, bing-bong; go to town where Mr. Long the store-man sells them gongs and tongs, go to church where they sing songs, families who, a day later when I am tired of them, have houses that catch on fire and burn to the ground, or with a sweep of the erasing cloth, like Germany, never existed at all.

*

Goodness gracious sake's alive!
How many fishes?
There are five.

This rhyme I tell my mother I like best. She thinks it is a funny one to like best. You would think I would like *Hickory dickory dock* or *Tom, Tom the Piper's Son*. But it is *Goodness, gracious sake's alive!* which I read over and over again as I stretch out over the Mother Goose book on the kitchen floor, a book of thick brown, dog-eared pages that my mother found in a bunch of messy papers in the bottom of the dresser drawer in my room upstairs.

"I don't know where it came from," my mother says.

But I do. Mother Goose flew over the house one night while we were sleeping, and put it there.

Goodness gracious sake's alive! I like the best, because it tells me about the time I have been waiting for all winter, the time I will 'turn' five in July. I can go to school when I am five.

"You are just killing time," my mother says.

"How do you kill time?" I ask her, imagining for a moment it is something like stabbing the clock on the warming oven with a knife. She smiles, opening her mouth just enough to show the gold tooth that she does not want to show. As if the gold tooth is the answer.

To kill time, my mother sometimes gives me magazines to read, old ones that Aunt Frances leaves behind in a big slidey pile on the oilcloth of the kitchen table when, once in a while, she comes in her car on a Sunday visit. She has a car because she does not have a husband and she is a teacher.

There are stories in the magazines my mother likes to read, and things for me to see: toothpaste, smiling ladies with bright red lips, bars of soap, cans of Magic baking powder.

One day, down on my knees on the cool linoleum, my head bent over one of Aunt Frances's magazines, my fingers having trouble turning its broad pages, there appears under me a spreading of something dark that looks like a large ugly crooked-legged insect.

"Mummy! what's this!" I ask, afraid.

She comes over from where she is stirring tapioca and takes a look down and draws in her breath.

"It's Hitler's crooked cross, his swastika," she says. "It was his sign to show he wanted to take over the world."

And she bends and takes the magazine away and goes behind the wood box and throws it in the cubbyhole and shuts the door.

"You don't want to look at such a thing," she says. "It's probably that article on Strasser."

But I am looking at it, shadowy swastika thing that is still there, that has somehow lifted itself off the magazine and is crookedly spreading itself outwardly over the kitchen floor, out through the windows, out through the doors, out to the outdoors of trees and orchards and hills and fields and mountains and bays, crooked-cross swastika spreading itself out across the oceans, out over the countries of the flags of the whole world.

"Don't worry, Sis, Hitler's not going to kill anybody any more."

Hitler, Otto's old friend, is dead. That is it for his terrible machine, that is it for the war. What my father who listens to Otto has said. But I am not so sure.

*

On another winter afternoon, when the stove is black hot and its silver elbows and knees are shining and the linoleum is smoothly brown and almost warm, when the kitchen's dull yellow-ribbed walls and doors close in around me cosy, and the chilly north-window at my back is frosted with sparkling white trees, I come across another strange page in a magazine.

"What's this?" I ask, wanting my mother to come out of the pantry and look and see this glossy page of coloured-complicated things, things that look to me like badges. But she does not come out, so I have to call again, several times, because it is a day she wants to get things done and I am to amuse myself and she does not want to answer.

"Mummy!"

Finally she comes out, holding the rolling pin.

"O those are coats-of-arms, shields," she says, looking down at them.

"That's a lion, that's a dragon...that's a deer."

"I know, I know," I say, not wanting her to explain everything.

"They're like badges," I say.

Like Uncle Everett's from the war, for being a brave soldier.

How are they shields? They are not like the shields Harold and Peter and I saw out of cardboard with a bread knife making unbearable squeaking sounds, so we can play sword-fight out on the lawn.

"That's a unicorn," I say pointing to a badge bigger than the rest in the middle of the page. But it is not like the unicorn running all around the town in the brown-paged Mother Goose book. Here, it is a shining little white horse reared up on its hind legs, a creature with a gentle face and a golden horn that points straight out of its forehead.

"Crests might be a better word for some of them," my mother says, gesturing with the rolling-pin so that flour sprinkles to the floor.

"What's this one?" I say, pointing.

This one down in the corner, a strange goldenbrown creature that seems to be dancing under a tree, a tree that has small red crosses caught in its green leaves, a creature reared up on its hind legs that has taloned claws and tilting courageous wings, that has a strange beaked-head, a daring eye that looks straight at me. Like it knows me.

"Oh, one of those fabulous beasts," my mother says. "Not an animal that exists."

I look up at her eyes that glow like blue pearls.

"A griffin," she says.

"Griffin," I repeat after her.

It is a name I like, that in my mouth feels like feathers, fur, claws. A griffin who does not exist, my mother says, but who seems alive. Who stares at me. Who knows me. Who feels alive in me inside.

Part II

—age five to six—

Long winter over. Then spring of seeping water and roads of muddy ruts, of palebrown puddles that show deep in the earth the light of palebrown skies. Then long days of summer playing wild galloping horses with the boys on the mountain, of playing cowboys and Indians with bows and arrows and guns.

Over our heads, following our every move, the brilliant eye of the sun, seeing me, little girl on the road, skip, hop, dance, jump, sun seeing everything I do, seeing me the day I have to take down my sunsuit and wet in the ditch, summer when Maxine has gone and Sylvestor for haying has come.

Winter, spring, summer, fall, seasons which I now find myself sliding and skipping and hopping through, dancing into along the road, singing songs of my own, making up rhymes about things going round-and-round-and-round like the old steel-rimmed wheel the boys and I roll swaying ahead of us over the gravel of the road, wheel going round-and-round-and-round with musical sounds...

In the fall, to school at last. On the first morning in clear September air, walking behind Harold, who does not want me to catch up, walking as fast as I can under the leathery darkgreen leaves of the oaks, past the heavily-appled rows of the orchard, up the long slope toward Palmers', pleased with the newness on my back of my good-smelling book bag, inside it, my new brown notebook scribblers, new shellaced pencil-case, new red and yellow pencils unsharpened, the smooth-white Ganong's chocolate box that contains my lunch.

Walking fast, wheezy-fast, noticing, as the days of fall go on, damp clusters of purple asters, chilled heads of goldenrod in the ditches either side. Every afternoon, leaving school early to walk home on my own, my footsteps in my new brown-tie shoes dampening down through the shade of the hollow, hardening up the hill, down past Palmers', down through the warmth and locust-silence of the roadside banks. Above, pure blue sky.

To school. And my mother is going to school, too. Because these days married women can teach, she says. And not take jobs away from the men. And it is the way it should be that every morning when I walk with my chocolate box lunch toward our school in Central Wilmot that I turn around at the line-fence to see my mother turn out of the driveway in our old Ford truck and bump away in the opposite direction toward her school in Lower Wilmot, she with her own chocolate box lunch sitting inside what she calls her Indian school basket. My father driving her, so that for the day he can have "the use of the truck", which means, after I am home from school in the afternoon, my father and I go bumping down the road to Lower Wilmot to bring her back again.

Only once in a while does my mother drive herself. Just as only once in a while does Mrs. Morrison, our teacher at our Central Wilmot School, drive herself, being brought most days by her husband from some place across the river. Mrs. Lulu Morrison, who my mother knows from somewhere else, who is a better driver than my mother because she knows how to back up, how to turn her brown coupe around in the schoolyard to park facing out. "Your mother doesn't know how to drive worth a damn," my father says, making fun of her to Harold. She answers that it does not matter whether she knows how to back up or not, since all she needs to know in the Lower Wilmot schoolyard is how to steer in a circle to drive out.

*

For a while in the large high-ceilinged room of the Central Wilmot school, I am slow to see Mrs. Morrison. I see Thelma Proudfoot, Ronnie Tompkins, Gloria Rafuse, Peter, Harold, Barbara Tompkins, and other big kids from up and down the road sitting at double desks, girls' side, boys' side, in rows. But I cannot see Mrs. Morrison.

She is up there somewhere. To the front of the black stove and its black pipe that reaches high into the gloom of the ceiling before it bends back over the older kids' heads and disappears into the wall of the woodshed. I cannot see her because I am down too low

114

within the hard curve of the seat, my feet in my new brown tie-shoes hanging down cold, my elbows in the sleeves of my red-knit sweater heaved up high, as high as the desk's scarred surface, as high as the painful tightness in my chest. Mrs. Morrison is up there somewhere, a smudged blackboard behind her teacher's desk, but I can only seem to see the bronze recess bell that rests on its edge.

It takes a while but slowly I begin to see her: when she is moving through bright patches of light that fall into the schoolroom from the windows along the boys' wall or where she is fumbling through the cupboard by the boys' door; or the times she goes over to the sink in the girls' corner for a jar of water, or to the girls' side blackboard, where her long arm in a button-cuffed sleeve reaches up with a piece of white chalk. I begin to see her move toward where we are down here, coming to stoop over us little kids, a woman with sloped-shoulders in a wine-coloured dress, a long face powdered pale, a head framed in a roll (like my mother's) of grey hair. Her voice, too, I begin to hear, a voice which my mother says is "put on," but which to me, whether she is reading to us from her hidden desk or standing close and looking down over us, sounds like a white petunia flower.

I am not at school long before my mother complains that Mrs. Morrison is not teaching me much of anything, and my father answers her saying leave it well enough alone and my mother answers him saying she supposes Lulu is good enough for doing childish things with little kids, but what about Harold.

"So?" Harold says.

"I like Mrs. Morrison just fine," I pipe up.

I am very interested to hear what they are talking about.

"I want them to learn something!" my mother says.

"I suppose you think I don't know anything," my father says, heading for the porch door with a snap in his eyes, saying he guesses he better get out and do the work in the barn.

"I don't mean you at all!"

"Let's get goin'," Harold says, scraping back his chair to go out with the men.

"I like Mrs. Morrison just fine," I repeat to my mother, going up to stand near her at the sink, where I try to look up at her face. Why does she not want me to like Mrs. Morrison?

"What's wrong with Mrs. Morrison?" I ask.

"She'd be fine, if she weren't so two-faced," my mother says.

Mrs. Morrison is something like the little girl who had a little curl right in the middle of her forehead?

"I don't think Mrs. Morrison is horrid," I say.

My mother does not say anything more, just turns on the hot water tap's thin stream of water, tosses into the white enamel dishpan a handful of soap flakes, which smell strong in my nose.

"I like school!" I protest.

*

I like school. I like roll call and saying "present" and singing *God Save the King* and *The Maple Leaf for Ever*. I like showing my folded hanky and nails, clean as I can get them, for health inspection. I like saying The Lord's Prayer, all of us bowed and murmuring safe in the school's shadowy high-ceilinged air. I like listening to one of the older kids read The Psalm.

"Don't be shy, Barbara," Mrs. Morrison says.

"Not so loud, Ina."

I know what it is to be shy. To be shy, and not want to answer. I am shy with Uncle Spencer, who says teasing things to me I do not understand. But, once I see her, I am not shy of Mrs. Morrison.

There is no need, my mother says, of being shy of Lulu. "If you know something, don't hold back."

I like going up to the front of the school, turning around not-shy to read in front of the teacher's platform. I like reading out loud from the primer, whole sentences. I like reading and copying down numbers in my scribbler book from the side blackboard, numbers that are for Thelma Proudfoot and Gloria Rafuse a year ahead of me, but which I also "do".

I like looking up at the blackboards to see all the numbers for adding and carrying and subtracting and borrowing and multiplying and dividing. I like working, bending my head over my desk, chewing strands of my hair, yummy hair that hangs forward out of the strain of my red barrettes. I like printing letters, even though my fingers ache from trying to do their best to keep within the printing book's wide lines.

My printing is poor. Mrs. Morrison writes in my report card to my mother. I need more practice, she says, to keep the letters within the lines. Letters that on the bumpy green surface of the Chautauqua Board with my stub of chalk I printed any-old-where, same shapes as on the screen above. But no matter how hard I try in my printing book, Mrs. Morrison always marks me the lowest mark of C+.

"Thelma keeps a lovely neat book," Mrs. Morrison says to the whole school.

"Piffle," my mother says crossly, looking at my copybook and seeing nothing wrong with it at all.

*

I like being in school, especially when everyone is doing seat work and Mrs. Morrison is up at her desk hidden behind the stove's cosy heat, the whole school room studious and quiet. Then I look up at the dark water-circles on the ceiling or to the blackboard at the front of the school that is covered with Mrs. Morrison's neat notes for the older kids, that we are not allowed to touch. I look around at the other kids bent beaver-busy over workbooks, me the only one looking up to see the snowy sills of the windows on the boys' side, the glistening flakes of snow falling lazy-down outside in the day's cold sunshine. I am here in this school in Central Wilmot, Annapolis County, Nova Scotia, and nowhere else. Why?

"I suppose Lulu has you colouring all day," my mother says.

"No," I say.

It is only in the afternoons, when Mrs. Morrison is hearing lessons with the older kids, that we younger ones are left to draw pictures with our crayons. The colouring we do in the afternoon is not like the colouring we do in the morning. I do not tell my mother about the colouring in the morning, the colouring of the line drawings which Mrs. Morrison has us copy down from the front blackboard for art, the very same ones I have seen on the Chautauqua Board, the cat made out of two circles with tiny triangles for ears, a thin loop for a tail, the umbrella (hard to draw the wavy line), the three perfect round balloons on a string for floating in the air. The balloons, very hard to do, because I cannot make perfect circles like Thelma and Gloria.

Colouring in the afternoon is drawing with crayons anything we like, as long as we do not turn around and whisper, as long as we do not ask for more than two sheets of brown hen's-egg paper.

"If you can't think what to draw, draw a picture of winter," Mrs. Morrison says.

What Thelma does at her desk, where she sits with Gloria, behind me. A picture I turn around to see that shows a winter day with a blue brook and a black tree, a winter day with brown grass, where, because she has a white crayon, a little snow has fallen.

"Very nice, Thelma," Mrs. Morrison says, coming down to see it.

I draw teepees with bright patches of colours all over them. While I am colouring the patches, I am thinking that I am sleeping in this tepee at night, black sky of stars overhead, me inside wrapped in cosy fur. Outside the teepee is a bright orange fire. I colour in the orange fire, I colour in the black sky and the yellow stars. Sometimes I draw mountains, paths, brooks, pretty flowers, big bright suns, blue houses, huge green trees. Mrs. Morrison never says "very nice" to me.

Some afternoons we make decorations, lanterns for the windows, starting with a blank sheet of paper on which we measure lines for stripes that we colour in alternating colours with pinched fingers, our mouths pressed tight, bearing down hard with our crayons for Hallowe'en, orange and black; for Christmas, red and green; for Saint Patrick's Day, emerald green and black. After colouring, Ina and Barbara help us who are younger to fold the sheets in half, cut down between the stripes so far, then unfold them, glue their sides together. After the glue is dry, we squat them, then glue on their matching coloured-paper handles. Colourful lanterns we have made, which the older kids place for us on the sills of the windows where they sometimes blow off in the draughts.

When I look up from my workbook, I see my lantern in the snowy light, beauty-red and holly-green, lantern for Christmas coming, to light the baby in the manger, to light the hooves of Santa's reindeer. Around the tops of the blackboards are the snowflakes other kids have made, airy, mysterious, lacy, that Mrs. Morrison has hung up for us on strings. I cannot work the scissors to cut them out. I cannot make snowflakes at all.

We do not make red-and-white lanterns for Valentine's Day. Although Mrs. Morrison, pointing her lips, says in her petunia voice that we can if we want to. Instead, we make drawings of red hearts and blue hearts with arrows striking through them. It is all right to have blue hearts, Barbara Tompkins says, because sometimes people are blue. That means sad, so sad they cannot hold up their heads. We give Valentines to let people know we care about them when they are blue so we can cheer them up.

I like Barbara Tompkins, even though she is long and lanky and her clothes smell like the old milk separator at home in our porch. I like her because she is nice to me at recess. I like her long braids of slippery pale brown hair. I like her because one noon hour she reads a story that Ina Bolivar does not want her to read because she wants to read it herself, about Saint Valentine who even though he was in prison was kind.

Oh, I love Valentine's Day! Because on Valentine's Day we must bring a card for everyone so that everything is even, everyone gets a card, everything works out. Each card a mystery of x's you have to figure out.

Mrs. Morrison says it is not appropriate to make purple and yellow lanterns for Easter. We make pictures of bumpy green hills and black crosses on the brown hen's-egg paper instead. This is because there is a green hill far away, Barbara Tompkins says, where Jesus rose from the dead. Nobody knows how He did it, she says. But I know how. It is like going out through the ceiling into a beautiful country, instead of spinning into the wallpaper into a blackness where you forget you were ever awake....

*

Why is there no day or season for plaid?

A thought I am thinking one cool spring evening when there is rain on the north window, and I am up a bit late and the kitchen is quiet with the stove's burning, and I am sitting at the table in my pyjamas, sipping sweet cocoa and eating toast that has on it marks that look and taste like scorched wire. My father is at the table with me, his chair scraped back, his black-haired hands gripping the day's newspaper, whispering into its grey-lined thinness as he shifts it back and forth in front of his face. My mother is in the pantry, leaning over the board that covers the flour barrel because the light of the hanging bulb in there is better for marking the Lower Wilmot kids' tests.

Why no day for the red plaid of my pleated skirt that I wear to school under my brown tweed coat? Why no day for my plaid hat, my red plaid 'Scottish' hat with its black ribbons and closely-shy black-feather badge that Aunt Helen has sent from those Turnbull people in the States. Thoughts I am thinking, while I am sipping and chewing, Harold gone upstairs.

"You look like a little Scottish girl. Mumma was Scottish," my mother said, looking down at me on the day the hat arrived, me looking up at her, hoping she will like its pretty upside-down-boat shape.

"Don't you like your hat?" she asks. "It'll go with your red plaid skirt."

"I like it," I say.

I do. Except in my stomach I have a feeling about plaid that is like a sick-shake.

"Mum! Why is there no day for plaid?!" Shrilly, I call to my mother in the pantry from my north window-chair. There is a day for Ireland, why is there no day for Scotland, the country shaped like a griffin-beast that I have seen on the map on the school's back wall? A map that, to me, seems made out of a huge sheet of dingy white adhesive, that every once in a while Mrs. Morrison rolls down and points at with a stick for Arnold Keddy in Grade Eight, everyone else in the school turning around.

"There's England, there's Wales. There's Scotland, there's Ireland."

Why is there no day for Scottish Red Plaid when there is an Emerald Green Day for Ireland?

"Mum!" Calling again. Making my father rattle his paper. Making my mother mumble something that sounds like "Rob and Burns Day". I do not want to know about Rob and Burns Day.

"I want to know about plaid!" I yell.

"Wait 'til I finish," my mother says, patient.

"Mum!" I shriek, making my father pull the paper down to his chin, his dark eyes darting a warning.

I wait, gouging the furry backs of my slippers off my heels on the rung of the chair. I wait, swinging my legs for my mother to finish her homework, for my father to go back to whispering to himself behind the paper's shifting pages. I wait, the dark yellow ribbed walls of the kitchen around me seeming to dim for the night, the stove to go cold.

"Mum," I call out again.

But not loudly.

"There!" she finally says. "I'm finished."

She comes out of the pantry, carrying her Indian basket to put it away for the night in the dining room, comes back into the kitchen, pulling tight the ties of her rosypurple bathrobe.

"Just another minute, Maree," she says, going to the wood box for a stick.

With her fingers barely clasping it, she pokes it into the round hole of the stove and clanks down the lid.

"Wish you'd think once in a while to give the stove some wood," she says to my father.

But he is whispering into the paper and does not say anything back.

He does not say anything back because this is the time of night my mother says things, standing with her back to the stove, her blue eyes thinking of things, her pale chin tilted high.

"Some things I can tell you," she says.

About people up there in Pictou County and Antigonish, where Aunt Edna is from, people up there of Scottish descent. I don't want to hear about Scottish descent. About the terrible mournful wailing sound that bagpipes make. About men who wear plaid skirts called kilts, plaid scarfs and hats. I do not want to hear anything about that.

"Then you'd better go to bed then," my father says.

"Mumma is of Scottish descent," my mother says.

I have already heard her say this.

Mumma, my mother's mother, is no longer in Aunt Edna's kitchen, is no longer sitting on the edge of her bed. She is now in a greyblue coffin under the earth that is soggy from rain. Her face is covered with white-puckered satin, her upper body is dressed in a greyblue dress, her lower body is hidden from the waist down.

"Mumma might have been Scottish, but she set a good table just the same," my mother says.

"No, she wasn't mean, I'll say that for her," my father agrees.

"Mumma had a terrible, terrible life. Poor woman."

My mother's blue eyes stare out to the opposite wall over my father's head.

"Your Grammie Grave's got the Irish in her," my father says, pulling the paper down to look at me.

Grammie Grave, my father's mother, who he knows I like. Who is not in the grave. Even though her name is Graves. Who is alive. Up East in King's County this dark rainy night. Alive in her house.

*

I love Grammie Grave, yes, I do. Even though Grammie Grave, when we visit her in her house Up East, seems a small grey-haired woman we hardly know and hardly say anything to. Just someone Harold and I watch as we sit on worn-wood chairs against a darkbrown ribbed wall, an ugly smell of old boots coming in on a draught from the porch. A small grey-haired woman who with quick legs moves from stove to table and back with a big brown teapot, stepping over what Mum calls "those big lunky boys of Lorimer's," who live some place close by and who seem to think they can come to Grammie Grave's house on a Sunday and spend the afternoon rough-housing on her kitchen floor—my grandmother stepping over them and their reddened, straining faces, their squirming and grunting and grimacing, as she passes a plate of hard sparkling ginger cookies, hands our mother and father cups of tea, tumblers of slurpy cream-coloured milk to Harold and me.

"Great lummoxes like that. And she doesn't mind!" my mother says.

"She's used to lummoxes," my father says with his glinty-wire grin.

This not the same Grammie Grave who visits us in the winter, who sits in the chair beside our kitchen stove in a black-and-red trimmed sweater and a black flared skirt, with tiny-ankled legs crossed over at the knees, one high-heeled, black shoe swinging toward the lightbulb, the other, toe-tipped-down, pressed to the floor. This visiting Grammie Grave seems smaller, not much bigger than me. She has a brown-wrinkled face that grins with teasing me about what I know and do not know, making me giggle by telling me she can do anything I can do better: skip rope, bend to the floor from the waist, play cards, knit lickety-split, run up and down stairs in her high heel shoes clickety-click, who sleeps with me, not slumping me to the middle of the bed, but staying over on her own side, who chases after me in her flannel nightgown all around the house, upstairs and downstairs and in the ladies chamber when I sneak out of bed first thing in the morning and steal her girdle so she cannot put it on.

"Why, you're a regular scallywag," she grins at me.

Oh, I like this Grammie Grave. Almost as much as Valentine's Day.

I like her when she knits, not like Maxine with long smooth-tapered fingers, but with knotted veiny fists that seem to hold together a woollen nest of needles with jabs and picks, all the while talking, bright black little eyes, bright as the sparks of the stove she sits by, talking, talking with a voice we never tire of that sounds like cracking Christmas walnuts. Grammie Grave, who, my mother says, glancing with a smirk of amusement at my father, "has the gift of the gab."

"She'd be a smart woman, if she were educated, if her grammar were better. She only had Grade Two."

"Or maybe I should be saying, if her grammar was better."

"Missus, it can't make a helluva lot of difference!"

"Oh, yes it does! It's the difference between being correct and incorrect," my mother says, with a sharp light in her eye, a tone in her voice that says she knows best.

"Who cares!" says Harold, who has come back downstairs and is listening from where he is lying on the floor reading the comics by the woodbox.

Why does everybody have to get mad about how to say words?

"Ennaways," Grammie Grave always says.

*

By the second year of school I have caught up to Grammie Grave. I have gone through the readers of Primer and Grade One and I am in the Grade Two reader with Gloria Rafuse and Thelma Proudfoot.

"Other than reading and spelling, what did Lulu teach you today?"

What my mother asks most afternoons when we are in the truck jolting home up the deep-rutted road from her school in Lower Wilmot.

I answer "Lots" because I do not want to say.

But, after supper, when she is hearing my spellings, I often tell her things. I want to tell her some things, as long as she does not say that Lulu by this time of year should be teaching something else. I want to tell her about Annapolis County and how a toy boat set free in the stream of our brook or Peter's brook, right here where we live in Central Wilmot, would be carried through the lower woods to the Annapolis River and down the Annapolis River to the Annapolis Basin and then out into the Bay of Fundy and, who knows, from there into the Atlantic Ocean. The same thing in Kings County, the very same thing, only the toy boat in the brook that runs in the hollow by Grammie Grave would be carried into the Cornwallis River and would go the other way, east, into the Minas Basin and then out into the Bay of Fundy and then, floating west keep on going into the Atlantic Ocean. It could. I have seen how on the Nova Scotia map.

"The two boats might meet!" I wonderingly think to say.

"Not likely," my mother says.

"They might!" I say, hurt she does not see what I mean.

Why couldn't they?

I tell her, have to tell her, about the verses all of us in the school have to learn by heart by Wednesday: a poem Mrs. Morrison has printed on the blackboard from a magazine, a poem about sparkling snow, pink at morning, shadowy blue at evening. Also Psalm 121, which I know from church. I have to tell her because she has to hear me recite the words:

> *I will lift up mine eyes to the hills*
> *From whence cometh my help.*
> *My help cometh from the Lord*
> *Which made heaven and earth...*

"Aren't you learning that at Sunday School?" my mother asks.

No. At Sunday School we are learning verses about Jesus, God's only son.

"Why would Lulu give you a psalm and a poem to learn in the same week?"

"I like it when Mrs. Morrison gives us poems and psalms," I say.

I like psalms. I like lifting up mine eyes to the hills. I like lifting up mine eyes to the hills of the mountain as I walk to school every morning, hoping to reach as far as Palmers' place before the Tompkinses catch up. I like lifting up mine eyes to the hills to the trees of the mountain, the dizzy yellows, the fuzzy greens of the hardwoods in spring: the cool dark greens of summer far above the road's sultry heat; the brilliant red and yellow and orange fires of the mountain leaves in fall; in winter all colours gone to grey, except for the snowy-white darkness of evergreens.

I also tell her, and not sure I want to tell her, because I have been keeping it a secret, that I am going to sing a solo when the music festival comes. The music festival way down in Annapolis Royal. I tell her one early spring day when the roads are miry and we are on the way home from Lower Wilmot in the truck.

"What did Lulu teach today?"

"Pieces for the music festival because we're going to Annapolis Royal."

Place where nobody in the school has ever been. Place twenty miles and more away. Where Champlain landed. And to get there we have to go around a round hill. And we are going to sing a song from the yellow book called The Ash Grove, a song which, when Mrs. Morrison plays it on the organ, sounds like a lonely and lovely place I am missing, that I already know.

Along a green valley
Where runs a clear streamlet,
O oft have I wander'd,
Down by the Ash Grove.

"We are going to be a royal school chorus," I say proudly.

"Rural," my mother corrects. "And how is Lulu planning to transport a whole school of kids down to Annapolis Royal?"

I do not know. But I am going to sing a solo about a robin and this is the way it goes. And I suddenly sing it, my secret song, as loud and clear as I can over the roar of the truck as it sways through the mud up the Lower Wilmot Road.

> *There came to my window one morning in spring*
> *A sweet little robin, he came there to sing.*
> *The song that he sang was much prettier far*
> *Than ever was sung on a lute or guitar.*

"That's just great, sis," my father says, braking to swerve around a hole, my mother saving me from hitting my head on the dashboard by clutching my arm.

"Sing it again," my father says, keeping his eyes on the road.

But I cannot sing again, even though there is a shine on my father's face that says he is very pleased with me. The mud of the road is getting deep and thick and he has to grind the gears down slow.

"When we get home and in the house," my mother says, steadying me, tightening her fingers on the thick tweed sleeve of my coat.

The kitchen we step into out of the mould-smell of the porch is cold. The fire is out in the stove, and bark and woodchips that Dad should have swept up at noon time are scattered dirtily over the worn brown of the floor.

"You let the fire go out," my mother says, annoyed, bending over the soiled porch mat to take off her overshoes.

"I want to sing my piece," I anxiously say, bending behind her at the mat's edge to undo the hectic fasteners of my rubber boots, having to sit on the floor to drag them off my shoes.

"Go ahead, sis," my father says.

With my floppy tweed coat still on, I stand in my stocking-feet in front of the kitchen table, with folded hands (like Mrs. Morrison has been teaching me).

"Let's hear it," my father says, moving by my mother in one big stride to lean back against the stove, outdoor jacket still on, cap perched on the back of his head to listen to my song.

"Just a moment!" my mother says.

She takes up her Indian school basket to put away in the dining room, on her way back grabs the broom from the sink-corner to stand with it in the middle of the floor.

"Go ahead," they both say.

But how can I sing when the kitchen is cold and we all have our coats on?

> *There came to my window...one morning in spring*
> *A sweet little robin...he came there to sing.*

I try to sing. I try to sing the first two lines. But I cannot. I cannot sing much above a whisper.

"I can't sing. I can't sing now."

There's something in my throat. Something tight. Something that wants to cry.

"Sing out! You just need to sing out," they say together.

"I can't sing out!" I say hoarsely.

"They won't be able to hear you in the big auditorium."

"Mrs. Morrison said not to sing loud!" I rasp.

Better to sing in a tiny voice, like a tiny sweet little robin. What she said.

"Now why would Lulu tell you a thing like that!"

"Your voice is as clear as a bell, sing out!" my father says.

"Never mind Lulu!" my mother says, starting to sweep up the chips on the floor.

"Yes, sing out, for God's sake, sing out!"

"When you go to the festival sing out!"

"Sing the way you sang on the way home."

"Or else no one will hear you."

"Sing out, you'll sing something beautiful."

Their voices are in unison, they are both nodding their heads. I will sing out clear as a bell, because they have asked me.

*

At Christmas time there are three school concerts in Wilmot, the one down in my mother's school in Lower Wilmot, the one in our own school in Central Wilmot, and the one in Upper Wilmot that I hear about at church from a girl who lives up there, Mary Elizabeth Calkin. She says theirs is going to be the best concert of all. It is going to be best because it is going to take place not down in their school room but in the upper hall, where they are going to have real angels, and where they are not going to have school-desks, but rows of chairs.

I tell Mary Elizabeth that my mother is making fudge for her school in Lower Wilmot, brown sugar fudge, maple fudge, chocolate fudge, coconut fudge, white divinity fudge and creamy darkbrown sugar fudge with walnuts. I also tell her that Mrs. Morrison at our school in Central Wilmot is practising us to sing "Hark the Herald Angels Sing" and "Deck the Halls with Boughs of Holly," because she knows how to pump the straps of the school organ.

I do not tell her that at our school we are only going to have pretend angels, girls dressed up in pale blue-dyed curtains and gold foil wings and that I am not one of them, because Mrs. Morrison thinks it is enough that I am in the Christmas acrostic and the only one in the lower grades going to be saying a long monologue.

"Enough, don't you think, for one little girl?" she says, her small eyes pointed at me pleasant, her grey head with its rolled-up hair shaking back and forth in a kind of tremor.

"Yes," I nod back.

But I want to be an angel.

"We have a piano in our upper hall," Mary Elizabeth says. "And Rosie Beeler plays it something beautiful!"

O, I want to hear the piano in the Upper Wilmot hall played by Rosie Beeler.

The monologue I am going to recite is from an old Christmas concert book of my mother's, from the time before she was married, a book with a cover half-torn off and a mouse-gnawed spine, that is stored in the lower drawer of the buffet in the dining room. It is a monologue she found looking through the book for pieces for her Lower Wilmot kids, and she wants me to learn it and say it at her Lower Wilmot School concert.

"So people can see you down there," she says. "I'll help you learn your lines."

"I want to learn them myself," I say. "I want you to hear the lines."

"Fine!" my mother says, with a funny snap to her eyes.

"I'll write a note for you to give Lulu," she says.

The note is to tell her that since I am saying a monologue in the Lower Wilmot concert, I may as well say it in the Central Wilmot concert, too.

The piece is about a little girl talking to her doll, which for me, my mother says, can be my Mary doll from last Christmas. A doll I do not like very much because, although her face of blue eyes and small red mouth is pretty, she has hard painted-on-brown hair and a red floral cotton dress so short above the floppiness of her stuffed legs that it shows she has no underwear.

The night of the Central Wilmot concert, because of things my father has to do last minute in the barn, we are almost late. He drives up the snowy road fast—the four of us stuffed into the truck's cab—swerves angrily into the school driveway. He cannot see in the darkness where he is going to park; there seems no place left among the shadows of the other cars and trucks; he is going to have a hell of a time getting out, he is probably going to get stuck. But he sees beyond the darkened front of the school a place over by the swings and with headlights lighting up the yard's snow, he turns the truck around and backs in.

"Don't see why Dad has to get mad," I say, upset.

"I don't either," my mother says, as we climb the girls' side snow-scraped steps, me holding the Mary doll wrapped in a soft, snug piece of blue baby blanket that my mother found in the bottom of the window seat at the last minute.

"Wouldn't hurt your father to be a gentleman once in awhile," she says as we open the door into the pitch-black cloakroom.

"I don't want to be late!" I whisper.

"Of course you don't," my mother says.

Keeping the door open, she holds my doll, so my arms are free to take off my coat. The light of the snow outside is just enough for me to see among the shadows of coats on the opposite wall a peg to hang it on.

"I won't take mine off," my mother whispers.

We stand for a moment at the schoolroom door, listening. What if everyone is already up on the platform ready to sing "Deck the Halls"? How will I get up there? We go in, brushing past the woodsy-smelling branches of the school Christmas tree, move forward into a murmuring warmth of faces smiling at us from shadowy walls and darkened desks, faces that glow with the fluttering light of candles placed on the sills of the night-time windows like softly-lit stars.

"Old Mr. Foster's here," my mother whispers. "Even old Mrs. Palmer."

Holding the bundle of my doll under my chin, I leave my mother's side. I cross in front of the stove's black heat to the other side, to the rows of chairs brought down that afternoon by Mr. Saunders from the church, where all the other kids sit in the fluttering light with grinning faces.

"Yer late," Thelma says.

Remembering first to do what Mrs. Morrison said, I place the bundle of my monologue doll beneath the rungs of the chair, then scramble up beside her.

"Oink," Gloria, who sits on the other side of Thelma, says. Gloria doing that funny thing she was doing when we were rehearsing in the afternoon. Making us laugh, pushing up the end of her nose to make herself look like a pig.

"Don't," Thelma says.

I look 'round at the boys who are snickering behind us. Harold already in his row, in his seat between Peter and Bobby Dunbar.

"I like your ribbon," Thelma whispers to me.

I put up my hand to touch the white satin bow that already feels too loosely tied to one side of my hair.

"Your dress is pretty," I whisper back, pushing out over my knees the folds of my new green corduroy dress.

Thelma's dress of shiny icy blue material is like the dress of a princess.

"Mine's for Christmas," I say, brushing again at its hard-to-budge thickness, leaning down to stroke my new white stockings, the smooth-rib of them, that cradle my shins.

"Nice," Thelma says.

"Nice," Gloria mimics, leaning over Thelma to "oink" again.

Thelma and I giggle. We cannot help it. I lean around Thelma to see that Gloria's dress is reddish brown plaid, the one she wears every day, but immediately sit back, because the murmuring warmth is going quiet.

I look up to see that Mrs. Morrison's head shows through the split in the curtains drawn along the front of the desk platform. She looks as though she has bedsheets bunched up around her chin. In a moment our concert is going to begin!

"Ladies and gentlemen, I ask your patience for another minute while we light our lamps."

A couple of people clap. I look about in the flickering light. My mother and father are seated in church chairs over on the far wall. They are not that visible among the other heads, but I can see the whites of my mother's eyes stretching to see who is here, and my father looking around to nod to someone at the back of the schoolroom. Beside him, right in next to the Christmas tree, are Mr. and Mrs Henderson and their big lummox boy, Roland. Roland who is not in our concert because he is in Milverton School for Grade Five.

The boy is not really stupid, my mother has said. "They just can't get anything into his head."

Mrs. Henderson, my mother's friend, seeing me looking over at her, bumps me a little nod that tells me she likes my dress, its thickness, its deep beautiful Christmas green, so that I brush at it again with the heels of my hands, snug and safe and honourable over my knees.

"Mumma's at the back," Thelma breathes into my neck.

I look 'round. I don't see Mrs. Proudfoot. I don't see Gloria's mother, Mrs, Rafuse, either. They are in behind somewhere.

I see Peter's mother who is sitting under the pictures of the King and Queen, her blonde hair falling to one side of her face because she is speaking to a lady who has a little girl on her knee, a little girl who has just moved into the old Fenerty place, where Otto and

Margarita and the Czech people used to live before they moved away. A new little girl with pale hair and a round face whose name my mother says is Faye.

"Oink!" Gloria says, leaning over Thelma.

"Don't do that!" Thelma says, in a loud whisper. trying to get her to behave.

I sit back to be good, but I shake with silent giggling and have to push my fists into my cheeks.

*

The curtains part again showing Peter's father, Mr. Saunders, standing on the platform, everyone laughing because he is so tall his head shows above the wire like a stiltman. With his grey-suited arm he lifts a large red lamp that looks like a cage that has an oily yellow flame inside. He ducks under the curtain wire so as not to scratch his head and steps to the schoolroom floor.

"Jesus!" Gloria says in a loud whisper.

Mrs. Morrison steps down after him, smiling as if she and Mr. Saunders have been up behind the curtain on the platform hiding. Turning away from him, she tip-toes toward us in the front row, a flashlight in her hand making a skirt of light along the floor. Under her arm are her Christmas concert books that are like my mother's, except their backs are not mouse-gnawed.

She comes to stand in front of me and Thelma and Gloria, while everyone claps. I do not think to clap because I am looking up at something red and glittery on the shoulder of her black dress, a burning red corsage of Christmas bells that touches her pale skin where her dress is open at the neck.

"Ladies and gentlemen."
"Our Christmas concert is about to..."
"But first..."

Mr. Saunders, with a swing of his lamp, wants to draw our attention to the Christmas tree in the girls' corner, that way over there in the lamp's uncertain light stands very quiet and shy, its wispy branches seeming wispier with our 'made' decorations, our miraculous snowflakes and tilting red-foil stars hanging on their long threads, our chains of pale knuckly popcorn, icicles made from droopy pieces of cotton wool that have had their ends dipped in blue ink (that I do not like); the flimsy glistening ropes of tinsel, brought by Barbara Tompkins, that loop about its lower branches. Up top, from our school cupboard, a silver-tinsel star.

Here and there among the shadowy snowflakes, twinkling in the candle light, Mrs. Morrison's "offering to the school" from her home: red and blue and gold ornaments, each of them a tiny glinting globe, some of them silver-corrugated at their centres like tiny headlights of cars. Our school tree. For which everyone gives 'a round' hand of applause.

"And also, before...."

Someone we should thank—Mrs. Morrison—who with her trembly head moves out from the organ stool to smile at the people behind us, coming to stand in front of us again in her black dress—pleated down the sides, I see—her black instep-cuffed shoes slightly pointing out. Far above—I feel shy to look at it now —her bright red bell corsage.

Corsage.

I like the thick sound of the word corsage.

"All the work she's done, let's give her a hand!"

Everyone gives a smacking loud hand.

"Oink," Gloria says.

With a snatching sound, Harold and Bobby Dunbar, who went up on the platform while Mr. Saunders was talking, pull back the curtains to show that where Mrs. Morrison's desk was this morning is, tonight, a cave, lit by Mr. Saunders' red hurricane lamp at the front and by two yellow oil lamps on plant stands at the back. Behind the lamps a faint message on the blackboard, words put up by Ina Bolivar at noon hour in coloured-chalk:

MERRY CHRISTMAS!

Quiet. The room is quiet, people breathing, a small cough at the back, we kids good and quiet. Only the stove snaps.

Mrs. Morrison, in the boys' corner at the organ, flashlight beaming on her music from a shelf, turns and nods for us in the front row to slide off our seats and start up. I look over at my mother. Is she seeing me in my Christmas green corduroy dress slipping down with a bit of a lurch from the church chair? But over in the shadows she is looking down at her hands.

We sing, take our turns, little kids, big kids, saying our pieces, alone, in rows, in duets, before the whole community of glowing, watching faces, the lights of the surrounding candles seeming to wave and dance with all we have prepared: our recitations, our fancy drills with big red and green star-dusted letters that spell out *Happy Christmas!* a letter for each of us in the school (mine the second 's' on the end) and the extra letter, the exclamation mark, brought up in a hurry by Ronnie Tompkins.

Then a play by the older kids about comical happenings that go on at home, then Ina Bolivar coming up in a darkblue dress to read aloud the Christmas story for our manger pantomime, Barbara being Mary with a baby-doll Jesus wrapped in swaddling clothes; Orry Bolivar, Joseph; Harold and Peter and Bobby, three kings in bathrobes wearing golden tinselled crowns; the littler boys, shepherds in rolled-up trouser legs under cloaks of towels, around their heads their father's ties; all the rest of the girls angels, in their long blue curtain dresses and scallop-painted golden wings; everyone in the school up there, except me, sitting alone down in the first row on my church-chair.

Then my turn, me holding my doll in the blue blanket from home that has a faint smell of mothballs, stepping up into the space of the vacated manger to say my monologue, Mr. Saunders putting a small rocking chair in place for me near the hurricane lamp, and handing me a picture, drawn on a piece of paper, of Santa Claus, so I may sit in my green corduroy dress and talk not to Mary, but to silly little girl Dorothy, (me remembering just in time to take the protecting baby blanket off); Dorothy, who in her short red dress sits on my knee and keeps interrupting me, me her mother, asking me for pieces of candy, while I am trying to show her a picture of Santa Claus, me talking to my little girl Dorothy and forgetting, almost forgetting, that anyone out there is listening, saying the words I have learned with "real expression," thinking while they are coming out of my mouth that I do not like the sound of the word candy and why does Dorothy not listen, why does she keep asking for silly candy when she could be seeing a picture of Santa Claus, forgetting, almost forgetting everyone, but remembering, when all the words are over, to stand with Dorothy and curtsy to the glowing faces, Mr. Saunders, saying to everyone:

"Now, let's give Marion another round of applause."

I look over at my mother and father, at my mother's eyes that look extra blue-bright, at my father's smile that more than all the other people in all the other rows lights his face, because of the extra glints of the wires in his teeth.

Then, the last chorus, us lining up on the platform, looking out once more at the shadowy faces of the rows, around the walls, faces that with the candles guttering on the sills seem more solemn now. Over in the corner, Mr. Saunders reaches behind the organ to snuff out a draughty candle, stands in close behind Mrs. Morrison to hold up the flashlight so she can see to place her carol book on the rack.

"That was good!" Gloria hisses at me around Thelma as we stand waiting for the older kids to file into the back row.

I wanted to be an angel though.

> *Hark the heav'n-born Prince of Peace!*
> *Hail the Sun of Righteousness!*
> *Light and life to all he brings,*
> *Ris'n with healing in his wings:*
> *Mild he lays his glory by,*
> *Born that man no more may die,*
>
> *Born to raise the sons of earth,*
> *Born to give them second birth.*
> *Hark! the herald angels sing*
> *Glory to the newborn King.*

Concert over, going to go home.

But we have to stay awhile longer.

For the Christmas tree.

As we take our places below the platform again, we hear a faint jingle of bells, then a louder jingle of bells, then a knocking at the door like the King of Perigord, then a scary bursting of someone through the girls' cloakroom door with a loud *HO! HO! HO!*

Santa Claus, a skinny Santa Claus in a red suit and a black belt and white cotton batten beard, in big black rubber boots swipes by the tree to stand in the middle of the schoolroom floor so that the little Faye girl at the back wall starts to cry under the picture of the King and Queen.

But not me. I do not cry because I know who this is. Not the real Santa Claus at all. Only a man from down on the Saunders Road whose name is Judson Tidd. Just him playing the part.

"What a surprise to see you, Santa," Mrs. Morrison says, as Mr. Saunders, holding his lantern high, lights her way along the front of the platform to follow after Santa to the Christmas tree.

"Youngsters, welcome Santa!"

"Welcome, Santa," we all say loud.

I do not want to say welcome when I know he is not the real Santa Claus. And I do not want him giving out the gifts that Mrs. Morrison made sure we put under the tree in the morning in case tonight we forgot, the gifts we kids are giving to each other in the draw—from me to Orry Bolivar a pair of navy blue socks that Mum found in a drawer, new last year from Aunt Frances but still way too large for Harold. Gifts that Santa—getting Mrs. Morrison to read out the names—now begins to distribute with a loud Har! Har! until everyone has a gift and Mrs. Morrison says she wants to play Santa, too, asking each of us in her best petunia voice to come forward to receive a gift from her, a cardboard gift-box of hard tack and ribbon candy (no fudge), a plump twig of smokeypurple grapes on top. Also for each of us, like my mother gave the kids in the Lower Wilmot school, a big bright round orange with a smell that's razor-sharp.

"Thank you, Mrs. Morrison."

Our gift to Mrs. Morrison, given to her from us by Mr. Saunders, is a large Pot of Gold box of chocolates.

"Very kind of you," Mrs. Morrison says with a little nod.

Then, out, out through the doors with everyone saying a bright goodnight as we find our coats and boots and scarves and mitts, out of the crowded darkness of the cloakroom into the night's pure snow, out to our trucks and cars parked along what seems a midnight row of bare-branched trees, out into the night air that smells clear and clean.

Harold and Mum and Dad and me, the four of us sitting up snug inside the cab, Dad humming "Silent Night" that Mrs. Morrison at the last moment said "Let's all sing before we leave"; Harold next to me with arms folded, holding his orange and his candy box, Mum holding mine, me squeezed out to the edge of the seat in my bulky coat, with my monologue doll, softly long-legged in her blanket, tight in my arms. Mum's arm around my shoulders, me being careful of my boots against the side of her good wool coat, us roaring out of the school yard ahead of the rest, heading along the road for home, our headlights showing up yellow along the road's snowy banks. Through the window on Dad's side the moon shining down on Palmers' fields, the moon like a shining white boat sailing along beside us through the black night sky.

Inside my mitt, in the white cotton batten of a very small box, my gift from Barbara Tompkins who had my name, a brooch-pin, a tiny green-glittery frog, her gift to me.

"Christ the Saviour is bor-orn," my father sings over the steering wheel. "Chr-ist the Saviour is born."

Dad happy. Harold sort of happy, too. Not digging me. Mum not quite so happy but holding me tight, not going to say anything.

Janet Parker Vaughan

About the author

Janet Parker Vaughan (née Kinsman) was born in Middleton NS, and grew up on an apple and dairy farm in the beautiful Annapolis Valley. After school days in Bridgetown, she graduated from Acadia University in chemistry, but later took up literary studies at Western University in London, Ontario. For several years she worked ecumenically and as an  officer of the Anglican Church of Canada in global advocacy and education. In this calling she had the great privilege of relating to justice communities across Canada and on three continents.

As a writer, she has taken a special interest in the recovery of the devalued feminine in local and global cultures. Her work is rooted in her fascination with the spiritual mystery of unfolding life in its suffering and joys, its patterns, cycles and syndromes.

Janet came home to the Valley to live in Middleton. Her daughter Suzy lives nearby. Her dear husband Edward is recently deceased.